Shakespeare's Christmas

ALSO BY CHARLAINE HARRIS

Aurora Teagarden Mysteries

Sleep Like a Baby

All the Little Liars

Poppy Done to Death

Last Scene Alive

A Fool and His Honey

Dead Over Heels

The Julius House

Three Bedrooms, One Corpse

A Bone to Pick

Real Murders

Lily Bard Mysteries

Shakespeare's Counselor

Shakespeare's Trollop

Shakespeare's Champion

Shakespeare's Landlord

Sookie Stackhouse Novels

After Dead

Dead Ever After

Deadlocked

Dead Reckoning

Dead in the Family

Dead and Gone

From Dead to Worse

All Together Dead

Definitely Dead

Dead as a Doornail

Dead to the World

Club Dead

Living Dead in Dallas

Dead Until Dark

Harper Connelly Mysteries

Grave Secret

An Ice Cold Grave

Grave Surprise

Grave Sight

Cemetery Girl Trilogy (with Christopher Golden)

Haunted

Inheritance

The Pretenders

Midnight, Texas Novels

Night Shift

Day Shift

Midnight Crossroad

Standalones

A Secret Rage

Sweet and Deadly

SHAKESPEARE'S CHRISTMAS

Charlaine Harris

MINOTAUR BOOKS

NEW YORK

SHAKESPEARE'S CHRISTMAS. Copyright © 1998 by Charlaine Harris. All rights reserved. Printed in the United States of America. For information, address St. Martin's Press, 175 Fifth Avenue, New York, N.Y. 10010.

www.minotaurbooks.com

The Library of Congress has cataloged the hardcover edition as follows:

Harris, Charlaine.
    Shakespeare's Christmas / Charlaine Harris.—1st ed.
       p. cm.
    ISBN 0-312-19330-0
    I. Title.
    PS3558.A6427S524   1998
    813'.54—dc21

                                                            98-21120
                                                            CIP

ISBN 978-1-250-10729-9 (trade paperback)

Our books may be purchased in bulk for promotional, educational, or business use. Please contact your local bookseller or the Macmillan Corporate and Premium Sales Department at 1-800-221-7945, extension 5442, or by email at MacmillanSpecialMarkets@macmillan.com.

First published by St. Martin's Press

First Minotaur Books Paperback Edition: October 2018

10 9 8 7 6 5 4 3 2 1

For Dean James: reader, writer, friend,
and bookseller extraordinaire

Acknowledgments

My thanks to all who gave me information and advice while I was writing this book: retired police chief Phil Gates, go-between Ann Hilgeman, private detective Norma Rowell, and fingerprint expert M. Nolte.

SHAKESPEARE'S CHRISTMAS

ONE

My situation was as surreal as one of those slo-mo nightmares Hollywood uses to pad B movies.

I was sitting in the bed of a moving Dodge Ram pickup. I was enthroned on a wobbly plastic lawn chair, thinly disguised by a red plush couch throw edged with fringe. A crowd lined both sides of the street, waving and yelling. From time to time, I dipped my hand into the white plastic bucket settled on my lap, coming up with a fistful of candy to pitch to the spectators.

Though I was clothed, which I understand is not the case in many dreams, my clothes were hardly typical. I was wearing a red Santa hat with a big white ball on the end, bright new green sweats, and I had a disgusting artificial holly corsage pinned to my chest. I was trying to smile.

Spotting a familiar face in the crowd, a face pasted with an unconcealed smirk, I pitched the next peppermint with deliberate accuracy. It smacked my neighbor, Carlton Cockroft, right in the middle of the chest, wiping off that smirk for at least a second.

The pickup paused, continuing a familiar and irritating pattern that had begun minutes after the parade had started lurching down Main Street. One of the bands ahead of us had stopped to blare out a Christmas song, and I had to smile and wave at the same damn people over and over until the song was finished.

My face hurt.

At least in the green sweats, with a layer of thermal underwear underneath, I was fairly warm, which was more than I could say for the girls who had enthusiastically agreed to ride on the Body Time float directly ahead. They also were wearing Santa hats, but below the hats they wore only scanty exercise outfits, since at their age making an impact was more important than staying comfortable and healthy.

"How you doing back there?" Raphael Roundtree called, leaning out of the pickup window to give me an inquiring glance.

I glared back at him. Raphael was wearing a coat, scarf, and gloves, and the heat in the cab of the truck was turned on full blast. His round brown face looked plain old smug.

"Just fine," I said ferociously.

"Lily, Lily, Lily," he said, shaking his head. "Slap that smile back on, girl. You're gonna scare customers away, rather than pick some up."

I cast my gaze to heaven to indicate I was asking for patience. But instead of a clear gray sky, I found myself staring at tacky fake greenery strung across the street. Everywhere I looked, the trappings of the season had taken over. Shakespeare doesn't have a lot of money for Christmas decorations, so I'd seen the same ones every holiday in the four-plus years I'd spent in this little Arkansas town. Every alternate streetlight had a big candle suspended on a curved "candleholder." The other streetlights sported bells.

The town's seasonal centerpiece (since the manger scene had to be removed) was a huge Christmas tree on the courthouse lawn; the churches sponsored a big public party to decorate it. In consequence, it looked very homey rather than elegant—typical of Shakespeare, come to think of it. Once we passed the courthouse, the parade would be nearly over.

There was a little tree in the pickup bed with me, but it was artificial. I'd decorated it with gold stiffened ribbon, gold ornaments, and gold and white artificial flowers. A discreet sign attached to it read, TREE DECORATING DONE BY APPOINTMENT. BUSINESSES AND HOMES. This new service I was providing was definitely designed for people who'd opted for elegance.

The banners on the sides of the pickup read, SHAKESPEARE'S CLEANING AND ERRANDS, followed by my phone number. Since Carlton, my accountant, had advised it so strongly, I had finally made myself a business. Carlton further advised me to begin to establish a public presence, very much against my own inclinations.

So here I was in the damn Christmas parade.

"Smile!" called Janet Shook, who was marching in place right behind the pickup. She made a face at me, then turned to the forty or so kids following her and said, "Okay, kids! Let's Shakespearecise!" The children, amazingly, did not throw up, maybe because none of them was over ten. They all attended the town-sponsored "Safe After School" program that employed Janet, and they seemed happy to obey her. They all began to do jumping jacks.

I envied them. Despite my insulation, sitting still was taking its toll. Though Shakespeare has very mild winters as a rule, today was the coldest temperature for Christmas parade day in seven years, the local radio station had informed us.

Janet's kids looked red-cheeked and sparkly eyed, and so did Janet. The jumping jacks had turned into a kind of dance. At least, I guessed it was. I am not exactly tuned in to popular culture.

I was still stretching my lips up to smile at the surrounding faces, but it was a real strain. Relief overwhelmed me as the truck began moving again. I started tossing candy and waving.

This was hell. But unlike hell, it was finite. Eventually, the candy bucket was empty and the parade had reached its endpoint, the parking lot of Superette Grocery. Raphael and his oldest son helped me take the tree back to the travel agent's office for whom I'd decorated it, and they carted the plastic chair back to their own backyard. I'd thanked Raphael and paid him for his gas and time, though he'd protested.

"It was worth it just to see you smile that long. Your face is gonna be sore tomorrow," Raphael said gleefully.

What became of the red plush throw I don't know and don't want to know.

Jack was not exactly sympathetic when he called me from Little Rock that night. In fact, he laughed.

"Did anyone film this parade?" he asked, gasping with the end convulsions of his mirth.

"I hope not."

"Come on, Lily, loosen up," he said. I could still hear the humor in his voice. "What are you doing this holiday?"

This seemed like a touchy question to me. Jack Leeds and I had been seeing each other for about seven weeks. We were too new to take it for granted that we'd be spending Christmas together, and too unsure to have had any frank discussion about making arrangements.

"I have to go home," I said flatly. "To Bartley."

A long silence.

"How do you feel about that?" Jack asked cautiously.

I steeled myself to be honest. Frank. Open. "I have to go to my sister Varena's wedding. I'm a bridesmaid."

Now he didn't laugh.

"How long has it been since you saw your folks?" he asked.

It was strange that I didn't know the answer. "I guess maybe . . . six months? Eight? I met them in Little Rock one day . . . around Easter. It's years since I've seen Varena."

"And you don't want to go now?"

"No," I said, relieved to be able to speak the truth. When I'd been arranging my week off work, after my employers got over the shock of my asking, they'd been almost universally delighted to hear that I was going to my sister's wedding. They couldn't tell me fast enough that it was fine for me to miss a week. They'd asked about my sister's age (twenty-eight, younger than me by three years), her fiancé (a pharmacist, widowed, with a little daughter), and what I was going to wear in the wedding. (I didn't know. I'd sent Varena some money and my size when she said she'd settled on bridesmaids' dresses, but I hadn't seen her selection.)

"So when can I see you?" Jack asked.

I felt a warm trickle of relief. I was never sure what was

5

going to happen next with us. It seemed possible to me that someday Jack wouldn't call at all.

"I'll be in Bartley all the week before Christmas," I said. "I was planning on getting back to my house by Christmas Day."

"Miss having Christmas at home?" I could feel Jack's surprise echoing over the telephone line.

"I will be home—here—for Christmas," I said sharply. "What about you?"

"I don't have any plans. My brother and his wife asked me, but they didn't sound real sincere, if you know what I mean." Jack's parents had both died within the past four years.

"You want to come here?" My face tensed with anxiety as I waited to hear his answer.

"Sure," he said, and his voice was so gentle I knew he could tell how much it had cost me to ask. "Will you put up mistletoe? Everywhere?"

"Maybe," I said, trying not to sound as relieved as I was, or as happy as I felt. I bit my lip, suppressing a lot of things. "Do you want have a real Christmas dinner?"

"Turkey?" he said hopefully. "Cornbread dressing?"

"I can do that."

"Cranberry sauce?"

"I can do that."

"English peas?"

"Spinach Madeleine," I countered.

"Sounds good. What can I bring?"

"Wine." I seldom drank alcohol, but I thought with Jack around a drink or two might be all right.

"OK. If you think of anything else, give me a call. I've

got some work to finish up here within the next week, then I have a meeting about a job I might take on. So I may not get down there until Christmas."

"Actually, I have a lot to do right now, too. Everyone's trying to get extra cleaning done, giving Christmas parties, putting up trees in their offices."

It was just over three weeks until Christmas. That was a long time to spend without seeing Jack. Even though I knew I was going to be working hard the entire period, since I counted going home to the wedding as a sort of subcategory of work, I felt a sharp pang at the thought of three weeks' separation.

"That seems like a long time," he said suddenly.

"Yes."

Having admitted that, both of us backed hastily away.

"Well, I'll be calling you," Jack said briskly.

He'd be sprawled on the couch in his apartment in Little Rock as he talked on the phone. His thick dark hair would be pulled back in a ponytail. The cold weather would have made the scar on his face stand out, thin and white, a little puckered where it began at the hairline close to his right eye. If Jack had met with a client today, he'd be wearing nice slacks and a sports coat, wing tips, a dress shirt, and a tie. If he'd been working surveillance, or doing the computer work that increasingly formed the bulk of a private detective's routine, he'd be in jeans and a sweater.

"What are you wearing?" I asked suddenly.

"I thought I was supposed to ask you that." He sounded amused, again.

I kept a stubborn silence.

"Oh, OK. I'm wearing—you want me to start with the

bottom or the top?—Reeboks, white athletic socks, navy blue sweatpants, Jockeys, and a Marvel Gym T-shirt. I just got home from working out."

"Dress up at Christmas."

"A suit?"

"Oh, maybe you don't have to go that far. But nice."

"OK," he said cautiously.

Christmas this year was on a Friday. I had only two Saturday clients at the moment, and neither of them would be open the day after Christmas. Maybe I could get them done on Christmas morning, before Jack got here.

"Bring clothes for two days," I said. "We can have Friday afternoon and Saturday and Sunday." I suddenly realized I'd *assumed*, and I took a sharp breath. "That is, if you can stay that long. If you want to."

"Oh, yes," he said. His voice sounded rougher, darker. "Yes, I want to."

"Are you smiling?"

"You could say so," he affirmed. "All over."

I smiled a little myself. "OK, see you then."

"Where'd you say your family was? Bartley, right? I was talking to a friend of mine about that a couple of nights ago."

It felt strange to know he had talked about me. "Yes, Bartley. It's in the Delta, a little north and a lot east of Little Rock."

"Hmmm. It'll be OK, seeing your family. You can tell me all about it."

"OK." That did sound good, realizing I could talk about it afterward, that I wouldn't come home to silence and emptiness, drag through days and days rehashing the tensions in my family.

Instead of saying this to Jack, I said, "Good-bye."

8

I heard him respond as I laid the receiver down. We always had a hard time ending conversations.

There are two towns in Arkansas named Montrose. The next day, I drove to the one that had shopping.

Since I no longer worked for the Winthrops, I had more free time on my hands than I could afford: That was the only reason I'd listened when Carlton had proposed the Christmas parade appearance. Until more people opted for my services, I had just about two free mornings a week. This free morning, I'd gone to Body Time for my workout (it was triceps day), come home to shower and dress, and stopped by the office of the little Shakespeare paper to place an ad in the classifieds ("Give your wife her secret Christmas wish—a maid").

And now here I was, involuntarily listening—once again—to taped Christmas carols, surrounded by people who were shopping with some air of excitement and anticipation. I was about to do what I like least to do: spend money when I had little coming in, and spend that money on clothing.

In what I thought of as my previous life, the life I'd led in Memphis as scheduler for a large cleaning service, I'd been quite a dresser. In that life, I'd had long brown hair, and lifting two twenty-pound dumbbells had made my arms tremble. I'd also been naive beyond belief. I had believed that all women were sisters under the skin, and that underneath all the crap, men were basically decent and honest.

I made an involuntary sound of disgust at the memory, and the white-haired lady sitting on the bench a yard away said, "Yes, it is a little overwhelming after a month and more, isn't it?"

I turned to look at her. Short and stout, she had chosen to wear a Christmas sweatshirt with reindeer on it and green slacks. Her shoes could have been advertised as "comfort-plus walkers." She smiled at me. She was alone like I was, and she had more to say.

"They start the selling season so early, and the stores put up the decorations almost before they clear the Halloween stuff away! Takes you right out of the mood, doesn't it!"

"Yes," I agreed. I swung back to glance in the window, seeing my reflection . . . checking. Yes, I was Lily, the newer version, short blond hair, muscles like hard elastic bands, wary and alert. Strangers generally tended to address their remarks to someone else.

"It's a shame about Christmas," I told the old woman and walked away.

I pulled the list out of my purse. It would never be shorter unless I could mark something off by making a purchase. My mother had very carefully written down all the social events included in my sister's prewedding buildup and starred all the ones I was absolutely required to attend. She had included notes on what I should wear, in case I'd forgotten what was appropriate for Bartley society.

Unspoken in the letter, though I could read the words in invisible ink, was the plea that I honor my sister by wearing suitable clothes and making an effort to be "social."

I was a grown woman, thirty-one. I was not childish enough, or crazy enough, to cause Varena and my parents distress by inappropriate clothing and behavior.

But as I went into the best department store in the mall, as I stared over the racks and racks of clothing, I found myself completely at a loss. There were too many choices for a woman who'd simplified her life down to the bone. A saleswoman asked if she could help me, and I shook my head.

This paralysis was humiliating. I prodded my brain. I could do this. I should get . . .

"Lily," said a warm, deep voice.

I followed it up, and up, to the face of my friend Bobo Winthrop. Bobo's face had lost the element of boy that had made it sweet. He was a nineteen-year-old man.

Without a thought, I put my arms around him. The last time I'd seen Bobo, he'd been involved in a family tragedy that had torn the Winthrop clan in two. He'd transferred to a college out of state, somewhere in Florida. He looked as if he'd made the most of it. He was tan, had apparently lost a little weight.

He hugged me back even more eagerly. Then as I leaned back to look at him again, he kissed me, but he was wise enough to break it off before it became an issue.

"Are you out of school for the holidays?" I asked.

"Yes, and after that I'll start back here at U of A." The University of Arkansas had a large campus at Montrose, though some of the Shakespeare kids preferred the biggest establishment in Fayetteville, or the Little Rock branch.

We looked at each other, in silent agreement not to discuss the reasons Bobo had left the state for a while.

"What are you doing today, Lily? Not at work?"

"No," I answered shortly, hoping he wouldn't ask me to spell out the fact that his mother no longer employed me, and as a result, I'd lost a couple of other clients.

He gave me a look that I could only characterize as assessing. "And you're here shopping?"

"My sister's getting married. I have to go home for the wedding and the prewedding parties."

"So, you're here to get something to wear." Bobo eyed me a minute more. "And you don't like to shop."

"Right," I said disconsolately.

"Got to go to a shower?"

"I have a list," I told him, aware of how bleak my voice sounded.

"Let's see."

I handed him the sheet of stationery.

"A shower . . . two showers. A dinner. Then the rehearsal dinner. The wedding. You'll be a bridesmaid?"

I nodded.

"So she's got your dress for that?"

I nodded again.

"So, what do you need?"

"I have a nice black suit," I said.

Bobo looked expectantly at me.

"That's it."

"Oh, wow, Lily," he said, suddenly sounding his age. "Do you ever have *shopping* to do."

That evening I spread out my purchases on the bed. I'd had to use my charge card, but everything I'd gotten I could use for a long time.

A pair of well-cut black slacks. For one shower, I'd wear them with a gold satin vest and an off-white silk blouse. For the second, I'd wear them with an electric blue silk shell and a black jacket. I could wear the shoes that went with the black suit, or a pair of blue leather pumps that had been on sale. I could wear my good black suit to the rehearsal dinner. For the dinner party I had a white dress, sleeveless, that I could wear in the winter with the black jacket, in the summer by itself. I had the correct underpinnings for each outfit, and I had bought a pair of gold hoop earrings and a big gold free-form pin. I already had diamond earrings and a diamond bar pin my grandmother had left me.

This was all thanks to Bobo's advice.

"You must have read some of Amber Jean's girls' magazines," I had accused him. Bobo had a younger sister.

"Nah. That's the only shopping wisdom I have to offer. 'Everything has to match or coordinate.' I guess I learned it from my mom. She has whole sections of clothes that can be mixed and matched."

I should have remembered that. I used to clean out Beanie Winthrop's closet twice a year.

"Are you living at home?" I had asked when he'd turned to go. I was a little hesitant about asking Bobo any questions that might pertain to his family, so strained was the Winthrop situation.

"No. I have an apartment here. On Chert Avenue. I just moved in, to be ready for the spring semester." Bobo had flushed, for the first time looking awkward. "I'm trying to spend some time at home, so my folks don't feel too . . . ditched." He'd run his fingers through his floppy blond hair. "How've you been doing? You still seeing that private detective?"

"Yeah."

"Still working out?" he'd added hastily, getting off dangerous ground.

I'd nodded.

He'd hugged me again and gone about whatever his errand was, leaving me to a saleswoman named Marianna. She'd homed in on us when Bobo had joined me, and now that he had left, she was stuck with me.

. . .

13

After I'd gotten over the sticker shock, it felt almost good to have new clothes. I cut off the tags and hung all the new things in the closet in the guest bedroom, spacing the hangers so the clothes wouldn't wrinkle. Days afterward, I found myself looking at them from time to time, opening the door suspiciously as if my new garments might have gone back to the store.

I'd always been very careful with makeup, with my hair; I keep my legs shaved as smooth as a baby's bottom. I like to know what I look like; I like to control it. But I don't want people to turn to look at me, I don't want people to notice me. The jeans and sweats I wore to clean houses, to bathe dogs, to fill some shut-in's grocery list, acted as camouflage. Practical, cheap, camouflage.

People would look at me when I wore my new clothes.

Made uneasy by all these changes, by the prospect of going back to Bartley, I plunged myself into what work I had. I still cleaned Carrie Thrush's office every Saturday, and Carrie had mentioned she wanted me to come more often, but I had to be sure it wasn't because she thought I was hurting financially. Pity shouldn't have any part in a business arrangement, or a friendship.

I had the Drinkwaters' house, and the travel agent's office, and Dr. Sizemore's office. I still cleaned Deedra Dean's apartment, and I was working more hours for Mrs. Rossiter, who had broken her arm while she was walking Durwood, her old cocker spaniel. But it wasn't enough.

I did get the job of decorating two more office Christmas trees, and I did a good job on one and an outstanding job on the other, which was a very visible advertisement since it stood in the Chamber of Commerce office. I used birds and fruit for that one, and the warm, hushed colors and carefully concealed lights made the tree a little more peaceful than some of the others I saw around town.

I'd quit taking the Little Rock newspaper to cut back on expenses until my client list built up. So I was in Dr. Sizemore's office, on a Tuesday afternoon, when I saw the creased section from one of the Sunday editions. I scooped it up to dump into the recycle bin, and my gaze happened to land on the headline "Unsolved Crimes Mean No Happy Holiday." The paper was dated two days after Thanksgiving, which told me that one of the office staff had stuffed it somewhere and then unearthed it in her pre-Christmas cleaning.

I sank down onto the edge of one of the waiting room chairs to read the first three paragraphs.

In the yearly effort to pack as many holiday-related stories as possible into the paper, the *Arkansas Democrat Gazette* had interviewed the families of people who had been murdered (if the murder was unsolved) or abducted (if the abductee hadn't been found).

I wouldn't have continued to read the article, since it's just the kind of thing that brings back too many bad memories, if it hadn't been for the picture of the baby.

The cutline under the picture read, "Summer Dawn Macklesby at the time of her disappearance. Summer has been missing for almost eight years."

She was a tiny infant in the picture, perhaps a week old. She had a little lace bow attached somehow to a scanty strand of hair.

Though I knew it would make me miserable, I found myself searching for the child's name again, in the column of text. It jumped out at me about halfway through the story, past the mother of three who'd been gunned down at an automated teller on Christmas Eve and the engaged convenience store clerk raped and knifed to death on her Thanksgiving birthday.

"Eight years ago this week, Summer Dawn Macklesby was snatched from her infant seat on her parents' enclosed front porch in suburban Conway," the sentence began. "Teresa Macklesby, preparing for a shopping expedition, left her infant daughter on the porch while she stepped back into the house to retrieve a package she intended to mail before Christmas. While she was in the house, the telephone rang, and though Macklesby is sure she was absent from the porch no longer than five minutes, by the time she returned Summer Dawn had vanished."

I closed my eyes. I folded the paper so I couldn't read the rest of the story and carried it to the recycle bin and dumped it in as if it were contaminated with the grief and agony implied in that one partial story.

That night I had to walk.

Some nights sleep played a cheap trick on me and hid. Those nights, no matter how tired I was, no matter what energy I needed for the day to come, I had to walk. Though these episodes were less frequent than even a year ago, they still occurred perhaps once every two weeks.

Sometimes I made sure nobody saw me. Sometimes I strode down the middle of the street. My thoughts were seldom pleasant on walking nights, and yet my mind could not be at peace any more than my body.

I haven't ever understood it.

After all, as I often tell myself, the Bad Thing has already happened. I do not need to fear anymore.

Doesn't everyone wait for the Bad Thing? Every woman I've ever known does. Maybe men have a Bad Thing, too, and they don't admit it. A woman's Bad Thing, of course, is being abducted, raped, and knifed; left bleeding, an object of revulsion and pity to those who find her, be she dead or alive.

Well, that had happened to me.

Since I had never been a mother, I had never had to imagine any other disasters. But tonight I thought maybe there was a Worse Thing. The Worse Thing would be having your child taken. The Worse Thing would be years of imagining that child's bones lying in the mud in some ditch, or your child alive and being molested methodically by some monster.

Not knowing.

Thanks to that glimpse of newspaper, I was imagining that now.

I hoped Summer Dawn Macklesby was dead. I hoped she had died within an hour of her abduction. I hoped for that hour she had been unconscious. As I walked and walked in the cold night, that seemed to me to be the best-case scenario.

Of course, it was possible that some loving couple who desperately wanted a little girl had just picked up Summer Dawn and had bought her everything her heart desired and enrolled her in an excellent school and were doing a great job of raising her.

But I didn't believe that stories like Summer Dawn Macklesby's could have a happy ending, just like I didn't believe that all people are basically good. I didn't believe that God gave you compensation for your griefs. I didn't believe that when one door closes, another opens.

I believed that was crap.

. . .

I was going to miss some karate classes while I was in Bartley. And the gym would be closed for Christmas Eve, Christmas, and the day after. Maybe I could do calisthenics in my room to compensate? And my sore shoulder could use a rest. So as I packed my bag to leave, I tried not to grumble any more than I already had. I had to make this visit, had to do it with grace.

As I drove to Bartley, which was about a three-hour journey east and a little north from Shakespeare, I tried to drum up some sort of pleasurable anticipation about the coming visit.

It would have been more straightforward if I hated my parents. I loved them.

It was in no way their fault that my abduction, rape, and mutilation had made such a media roar that my life, and theirs, had changed even more than was inevitable.

And it was in no way their fault that no one I'd grown up with seemed to be able to treat me as a normal person, after that second, public, rape in the spotlight of the press and the TV cameras.

Nor was it my parents' fault that my boyfriend of two years had quit seeing me after the press turned their attention away from him.

None of it was their fault—or mine—but it had permanently altered the relationships between us. My mother and father couldn't look at me without thinking of what had happened to me. They couldn't talk to me without it coloring the most commonplace conversation. My only sibling, Varena, who had always been more relaxed and elastic than I had, had never been able to understand why I didn't recover more swiftly and get on with my life as it had been before; and my parents didn't know how to get in contact with the woman I'd become.

Weary of scrambling through this emotional equivalent of a hamster exercise wheel, I was nearly glad to see the outskirts of Bartley—the poor rickety homes and marginal businesses that blotch the approach to most small towns.

Then I was rolling past the filling station where my parents gassed their cars; past the dry cleaner where Mother took their coats; past the Presbyterian church they'd attended all their lives, where they'd been baptized, married, christened their daughters, from which they would be buried.

I turned down the familiar street. On the next block, the house I grew up in was wearing its winter coat. The rosebushes had been trimmed back. The smooth grass of the big yard was pale after the frost. The house sat in the middle of the large lot, surrounded by my father's rose beds. A huge Christmas wreath made from twined grapevines and little gold toy trumpets hung on the front door, and the decorated tree was visible in the big picture window in the living room. Mom and Dad had repainted the house when Varena and Dill got engaged, so it was gleaming white for the wedding festivities.

I parked to the side of the driveway on a concrete apron my parents had poured when Varena and I began driving. We'd had friends over all the time, and my folks got tired of their own vehicles getting blocked in.

I eased out of my car and looked at the house for a long moment, stretching my legs after the drive. It had seemed so big when I'd lived in it. I had always felt so lucky to grow up in this house.

Now I saw a fairly typical built-in-the-fifties house, with a double garage, a living room, a den, a big kitchen, a dining room, and three bedrooms, two baths.

There was a workroom at the back of the garage for my father—not that he ever did anything in it, but men needed a workroom. Just like there was a sewing machine in the corner of my parents' bedroom, because a woman ought to have a sewing machine—not that my mother ever sewed more than a ripped seam. And we Bards had a full complement of family silver—not that we ever ate with it. Someday, in the course of time, Varena and I would divide that silver between us, and the care of it would be on our shoulders; that heavy, ornate silver that was too fine and too much trouble to use.

I got my suitcase and my hanging bag out of the backseat and went up to the front door. My feet felt heavier with every step.

I was home.

Varena answered the door, and we gave each other a quick look of assessment and a tentative hug.

Varena was looking good.

I had been the prettier when we were girls. My eyes are bluer, my nose is straighter, my lips are fuller. But that doesn't have much meaning for me anymore. I think it still matters very much to Varena. Her hair is long and naturally a redder brown than mine had been. She wears blue contacts, which intensify her eye color to an almost bizarre extent. Her nose turns up a little, and she is about two inches shorter, with bigger breasts and a bigger bottom.

"How is the wedding process?" I asked.

She widened her eyes and made her hands tremble. On edge.

Beyond her, I could see the tables that had been set up to accommodate the presents.

"Wow," I said, shaking my head in acknowledgment of the sight. There were three long tables (I was sure my folks had borrowed them from the church) draped in gleaming white tablecloths, and every inch was covered with consumer goods. Wineglasses, cloth napkins and tablecloths, china, silver—more silver—vases, letter openers, picture albums, knives and cutting boards, toasters, blankets . . .

"People are being so sweet," Varena said, and I could tell that was her stock response; not that she didn't mean it, but I was sure she'd said that over and over and over to visitors.

"Well, no one's ever had to spend anything on us, have they?" I observed, raising my eyebrows. Neither Varena or I had ever been married, unlike some in our high school circles who'd been divorced twice by now.

My mother came into the living room from the den. She was pale, but then she always is, like me. Varena likes to tan, and my father does inevitably; he'd rather be out working in the yard than almost anything.

"Oh, sugar!" my mother said and folded me to her. My mother is shorter than me, bone-thin, and her hair is such a faded blond it's almost white. Her eyes are blue like every member of our family's, but their color seems to have faded in the past five or six years. She's never had to wear glasses, her hearing is excellent, and she beat breast cancer ten years ago. She doesn't wear clothes that are at all trendy or fashionable, but she never looks frumpy, either.

The months, the years, seemed to dissolve. It felt like I'd seen them yesterday.

"Where's Dad?" I asked.

"He's gone down to the church to get another table," Varena explained, trying not to smile too broadly. My mother suppressed the curve of her own lips.

"Is he rolling in this wedding stuff?"

"You know it," Varena said. "He just loves it. He's been waiting for this for years."

"This'll be the wedding of the decade in Bartley," I said.

"Well," Varena began, as we all started down the hall to my old room, "if Mrs. Kingery can get here, it may be." Her voice sounded a little whiny, a bit flat, as though this worry or complaint were so long-standing she'd worn out the emotion behind it.

"Dill's mother may not come?" I asked, incredulous. "So, she's really old and sick . . . or what?"

My mother sighed. "We can't quite decide what the problem is," she explained. She stared off into the distance for a moment, as if the clue to Varena's future mother-in-law's behavior was written on the lawn outside the window.

Varena had taken my hanging bag and opened the closet to hook the hangers over the rod. I put my suitcase on the triple dresser that had been my pride and joy at age sixteen. Varena looked back at me over her shoulder.

"I think," she said, "that maybe Mrs. Kingery was just so crazy about Dill's first wife that she hates to see her replaced. You know, with Anna being their child, and all."

"Seems to me like she'd be glad that Anna's going to have such a good stepmother," I said, though in truth, I'd never thought what kind of stepmother Varena would make.

"That would be the sensible attitude." My mother sighed. "I just don't know, and you can't ask point-blank."

I could. But I knew they wouldn't want me to.

"She'll have to come to the rehearsal, right?"

22

My mother and my sister looked anxiously at each other.

"We think she will," Varena said. "But Dill can't seem to tell me what that woman will do."

Dill (Dillard) Kingery's mother was still in Dill's hometown, which I thought was Pine Bluff.

"How long have you been dating Dill?" I asked.

"Seven years," Varena said, smiling brightly. This, too, was obviously a question that had been asked many times since Varena and Dill had announced their engagement.

"Dill is older than you?"

"Yeah, he's even older than you," my sister said.

Some things never change.

We heard my father's yell from the front door. "One a you come help me with this damn thing?" he bellowed.

I got there first.

My father, who is stocky and short and bald as an eight ball, had hauled the long table out of the bed of his pickup to the front door and definitely needed help getting it up the steps.

"Hey, pigeon," he said, his smile radiant.

I figured that would fade soon enough, so I hugged him while I could. Then I lifted the front of the table, which he'd propped against the iron railing that bordered the steps up to the front door.

"You sure that's not too heavy for you?" Dad fussed. He had always had the delusion that the attack I'd endured somehow had made me weak internally, that I was now frail in some invisible manner. The fact that I could bench-press 120 pounds, sometimes more, had no influence on this delusion.

"I'm fine," I said.

He picked up the rear of the table, which was the kind

with metal legs that fold underneath for easy carrying. With a little maneuvering, we got it up the steps and into the living room. While I held the table on its side, he pulled out the metal legs and locked them into place. We swung the table upright. The whole time he worried out loud about me doing too much, straining myself.

I began to get that tight, hot feeling behind my eyes.

My mother appeared in the nick of time with yet another spotless white tablecloth. Without speaking she shook it out. I took the loose end, and together we spread it evenly over the table. My father talked the whole time, about the number of wedding presents Varena and Dill had gotten, about the number of wedding invitations they'd sent, about the acceptances they'd received, about the reception . . .

I eyed him covertly while we transferred some of the crowded presents to the new table. Dad didn't look good. His face seemed redder than it should have been, his legs seemed to be giving him pain, and his hands shook a little. I knew he'd been diagnosed with high blood pressure and arthritis.

There was an awkward pause, once we'd gotten our little task accomplished.

"Ride over to my apartment with me and see the dress," Varena offered.

"OK."

We got in Varena's car for the short drive over to her apartment, which was a small yellow cottage to the side of a big old yellow house where Emory and Meredith Osborn lived with their little girl and a new baby, Varena explained.

"When the Osborns bought this house from old Mrs. Smitherton—she had to go into Dogwood Manor, did I tell you?—I was worried they'd raise the rent, but they didn't.

I like them both, not that I see them that much. The little girl is cute, always got a bow in her hair. She plays with Anna sometimes. Meredith keeps Anna and the O'Sheas' little girl after school, now and then."

I thought I remembered that the O'Sheas were the Presbyterian minister and his wife. They'd come after I'd begun living in Shakespeare.

Varena was chattering away, as if she could hardly wait to fill me in on all the details of her life. Or as if she were uncomfortable with me.

We pulled into the driveway and passed the larger house to park in front of Varena's place. It was a copy of the house in miniature, done in pale yellow siding with dark green shutters and white trim.

A little girl was playing the yard, a thin child with long brown hair. Sure enough, a perky red-and-green bow was clipped right above her bangs. On this cold day, she was wearing a sweatsuit topped by a coat and earmuffs, but still she looked chilly. She waved as Varena got out of her car.

"Hey, Miss Varena," she called politely. She held a ball in her hands. When I got out of the passenger's door, she stared at me with curiosity.

"Eve, this is my sister, Lily." Varena turned to me. "Eve has a sister, too, a new one."

"What's her name?" I asked, since that seemed indicated. I am very uneasy around children.

"Jane Lilith," Eve mumbled.

"That's pretty," I said, because I couldn't think of anything else to say.

"Is your sister taking a nap right now?" Varena asked.

"Yeah, and my mom too," the girl said forlornly.

"Come in and see my dress," Varena invited.

Eve really brightened up. Varena seemed to have a way with children. We trailed into the little front room of the house and followed Varena back to her bedroom. The closet door was open, and the wedding dress, swathed in plastic, was hanging on a special hanger that fitted over the top of the door.

Well, it was white and it was a wedding dress.

"It's beautiful," I said instantly. I am not stupid.

Eve was awestruck. "Oooo," she said breathlessly.

Varena laughed, and as I looked at my sister, I saw how warm and responsive her face was, how good-natured she looked. "I'm glad you like it," she said and went on talking to the child in an easy way that was totally beyond me.

"Can you pick me up so I can see the scarf?" Eve asked Varena.

I looked where the child was pointing. The veil, yards and yards of it, attached to an elaborate sort of tiara, was in a separate bag attached to the one holding the dress.

"Oh, honey, you're too big for me to pick up," Varena said, shaking her head. I could feel my eyebrows crawl up. Was it possible Varena couldn't lift this girl? I assessed the child. Seventy-five pounds, tops. I squatted, wrapped my arms around her hips, and lifted.

Eve squealed with surprise and delight. She turned to look down at me.

"Can you see?" I asked.

Eve examined the veil, admired the glittering sequined tiara, and went all dreamy-eyed for a minute or two.

"You can put me down now," she said eventually, and I gently lowered her to the floor. The girl turned to give me a long stare of evaluation.

"You're really strong," she said admiringly. "I bet nobody messes with you."

I could practically taste Varena's sudden silence.

"No," I told the little girl. "Nobody messes with me now."

Eve's narrow face turned thoughtful. She thanked Varena for showing her the dress and veil in a perfectly polite way, but she seemed almost abstracted as she said she'd better be getting home.

Varena saw Eve out. "Oh, Dill's here!" she exclaimed in a happy voice. I stared at the frothy white construction of a dress for a moment more before I followed Varena to the living room.

I'd known Dill Kingery since he moved to Bartley. He'd just begun dating Varena when the whole eruption in my life had occurred. He'd been a great solace to my sister during that time, when the whole family had needed all the help we could get.

They'd continued dating ever since. It had been a long engagement, long enough for Varena to bear a good amount of teasing from her coworkers at the tiny Bartley hospital.

Looking at Dill now, I wondered why he'd dragged his feet. I didn't think he'd been beating other women off with a stick. Dill was perfectly nice and perfectly pleasant, but you wouldn't turn to look at him twice on the street. My sister's fiancé had thinning sandy hair, attractive brown eyes, wire-rimmed glasses, and a happy smile. His daughter, Anna, was another skinny little eight-year-old, with thick, shoulder-length brown hair that was lighter than her father's. Anna had her dad's eyes and smile. Anna's mother had died when Anna was about eighteen months old, Dill had told us, in a car accident.

I watched while Anna hugged Varena. She was about to run to play with Eve when Dill stopped her. "Say hi to your aunt Lily," he said firmly.

"Hey, Aunt Lily," Anna said and gave me a casual wave of the hand, which I returned. "Can I play with Eve now, Daddy?"

"OK, sweetie," Dill said, and the two girls clattered outside while Dill turned to me to give me a hug. I had to endure it, so I did, but I'm not a casual toucher. And I hadn't quite adjusted to being "Aunt Lily."

Dill asked me the usual questions you ask of someone you haven't seen in while, and I managed to answer civilly. I was tensing up already, and nothing had happened to make me so. What was wrong with me? I stared out the front window while Dill and my sister talked over the plans for the evening. Tonight, I gathered, Dill was attending his bachelor dinner, while Varena and I and Mother were going to a wedding shower.

As I watched the two little girls playing on the front lawn, heaving the beach ball back and forth between them and running a lot, I tried to recall playing with Varena like that. Surely we had? But I couldn't dredge up a single recollection.

Without asking me, Dill told Varena he'd run me home so she could start getting ready. I looked at my watch. If Varena needed three hours to get ready for a party, she needed help, in my opinion. But Varena seemed pleased with Dill's offer, so I went outside to stand by Dill's Bronco. A tiny, thin woman had come outside of the bigger house to call to Eve.

"Hey," she said when she noticed me.

"Hello," I said.

Eve came running up, Anna in tow.

"This is Varena's sister, Mama," she said. "She came for the wedding. Miss Varena showed me her dress, and Miss Lily picked me up so I could see the veil. You wouldn't believe how strong Miss Lily is! I bet she can lift a horse!"

"Oh, my goodness," said Eve's mama, her thin face transformed by a sweet smile. "I better say hello, then. I'm Eve's mother, as I'm sure you figured. Meredith Osborn."

"Hello again," I said. "Lily Bard." This woman had just had a baby, according to Varena, but she looked no larger than a child herself. Losing "baby weight" was not going to be a problem for Meredith Osborn. I didn't think Meredith Osborn was over thirty-one, my age, and she might be even younger.

"Can you pick us both up, Miss Lily?" Eve asked, and my niece-to-be suddenly looked much more interested in me.

"I think so," I said and bent my knees. "One on either side, now!"

The girls each picked a side, and I hooked my arms around them and stood, making sure I was steady. The girls were squealing with excitement. "Hold still," I reminded them, and they stopped the thrashing that I had worried would topple us all over onto the driveway.

"We're queens of the world," Anna shouted extravagantly, sweeping her arm to indicate her turf. "Look at how high up we are!"

Dill had been talking to Varena in the doorway, but now he glanced over to find out what Anna was doing. His face looked almost comical with surprise when he saw the girls.

With the anxious smile of someone who is trying not to panic, he strode over. "Better get down, sweetie! You're a big load for Miss Lily."

"They're both small," I said mildly and surrendered Anna to her dad. I swung Eve in front of me and set her down gently. She grinned up at me. Her mother was looking at her with that smile of love women get when they look at their kids. A little mewling sound came from the house. "I hear your sister crying," Meredith Osborn said wearily. "We better go in and see. Good-bye, Miss Bard, nice to meet you."

I nodded at Meredith and gave Eve a little smile. Her brown eyes, peering up at me, looked enormous. She grinned at me, a smile stretching from one ear to another, and dashed in after her mother.

Anna and her father were already in the Bronco, so I climbed in, too. Dill chatted all the way back to my parents' home, but I half tuned him out. I had already talked to more people today than I normally spoke to in three or four days in Shakespeare. I was out of the habit of chitchat.

I got out at my folks' with a nod to Dill and Anna and strode into the house. My mother was fluttering around the kitchen, trying to get something ready for us to eat before we went to the shower. My dad was in the bathroom getting ready for the bachelor dinner.

My mother was worried that some of Dill's friends might get carried away and have a stripper perform at the party. I shrugged. My father wouldn't be mortally offended.

"It's your dad's blood pressure I'm really worried about," Mom said with a half smile. "If a naked woman popped out of a cake, no telling what might happen!"

I poured iced tea and set the glasses on the table. "It

doesn't seem too likely that anyone will do that," I said, because she was looking for reassurance. "Dill's not a kid, and it's not his first marriage. I don't think any of his local friends are likely to get that carried away." I sat down at my place.

"You're right," Mom said with some relief. "You always have such good sense, Lily."

Not always.

"Are you . . . seeing anyone . . . now, honey?" Mom asked gently.

I stared up at her as she hovered over the table, plates in her hands. I almost said no automatically.

"Yes."

The fleeting look of sheer relief and pleasure that flashed across my mother's pale, narrow face was so intense I felt like taking back my yes. I was feeling my way with Jack every hour we were together, and to have our relationship classified as a standard dating situation made me horribly anxious.

"Can you tell me a little about him?" Mom's voice was calm, her hands steady as she set the plates down at our places. She sat down across from me and began to stir sugar into her tea.

I had no idea what to say.

"Oh, that's all right, I don't want to intrude on your privacy," she said after a moment, flustered.

"No," I said just as quickly. It seemed awful to me that we were so leery of each other's every word and silence. "No, that's . . . no, it's OK. He . . ." I pictured Jack, and a tide of longing swept over me, so intense and painful that it took my breath away. After it ebbed, I said, "He's a private detective. He lives in Little Rock. He's thirty-five."

My mother put her sandwich down on her plate and began smiling. "That's wonderful, honey. What's his name? Has he been married before?"

"Yes. His name is Jack Leeds."

"Any kids?"

"No."

"That's easier."

"Yes."

"Though I know little Anna so well now, at first when Dill and Varena began dating . . . Anna was so little, not even toilet trained, and Dill's mother didn't seem to want to come to take care of Anna, though she was a cute little toddler. . . ."

"That worried you?"

"Yes," she admitted, nodding her faded blond head. "Yes, it did. I didn't know if Varena could handle it. She never enjoyed baby-sitting very much, and she never talked about having babies, like most girls do. But she and Anna seemed to take to each other just fine. Sometimes she gets fed up with Anna's little tricks, and sometimes Anna reminds Varena that she isn't her real mother, but for the most part they get along great."

"Dill wasn't in the car wreck that killed his wife?"

"No, it was a one-car accident. Evidently, Judy, his wife, had just dropped off Anna at a sitter's."

"That was before Dill moved here?"

"Yes, just a few months before. He'd been living up northwest of Little Rock. He says he felt he just couldn't bear to raise Anna there, every day having to pass the spot where his wife died."

"So he moves to a town where he doesn't know a soul, where he doesn't have any family to help him raise Anna." I spoke before I thought.

32

My mother gave me a sharp look. "And we're mighty glad he did," she said firmly. "The pharmacy here was up for sale, and it's been wonderful to have it open, so we have a choice." There was a chain pharmacy in Bartley, too.

"Of course," I said, to keep the peace.

We finished our meal in silence. My father stomped through on his way out the kitchen door to his car, grousing the whole time about not fitting in at a bachelor dinner. We could tell he was really gleeful about being invited. He had a wrapped present tucked under his arm, and when I asked what it was, his face turned even redder. He pulled on his topcoat and slammed the back door behind him without answering.

"I suspect he bought one of those nasty gag gifts," Mom said with a little smile as she listened to Father back out of the driveway.

I loved getting surprised by my mother. "I'll do the dishes while you get ready," I said.

"You need to try on your bridesmaid dress!" she said abruptly as she was rising to leave the kitchen.

"Right now?"

"What if we need to take it up?"

"Oh . . . all right." This was not a moment I'd anticipated with any pleasure. Bridesmaids' dresses are notorious for being unusable, and I'd paid for this one as a good bridesmaid should. But I hadn't seen it yet. I had a horrible, wincing moment of picturing the dress as red velvet with fake fur trim to suit the Christmas motif.

I should have had more trust in Varena. The dress, which was hanging in my bedroom closet swathed in plastic like Varena's own dress, was deep burgundy velvet, with a band of matching satin ribbon sewed under the breasts. In back, where the edges of the ribbon came together, there was a matching bow—but it was detachable. The dress had a high neckline but was cut low in the back. My sister didn't want her bridesmaids demure, that was for sure.

"Try it on," Mother urged. I could tell she wouldn't be happy until I did. With my back to her, I pulled off my shirt and wriggled out of my shoes and jeans. But I had to turn to face her to get the dress, which she'd been divesting of its plastic bag.

Every time, the impact of my scars hit her in the heart. She took a deep, ragged breath and handed me the dress, and I got it over my head as quickly as possible. I turned so she could zip me, and together we looked at it in the mirror. Both our pairs of eyes went immediately to the neckline. Perfect. Nothing showed. Thank you, Varena.

"It looks beautiful," Mother said stoutly. "Stand up straight, now." (As if I slouched.) The dress did fit well, and who doesn't love the feel of velvet?

"What kind of flowers are we carrying?"

"The bridesmaids' bouquets are going to be long sprays of glads and some other stuff," Mother said, who strictly left the gardening to my father. "You're the maid of honor, you know."

Varena hadn't seen me in three years.

This wasn't just a wedding, then. This was a full-scale family reconciliation.

I was willing, but I didn't know if I was able. Plus, I hadn't been to a wedding in a long time.

"Do I have to do anything special?"

"You have to carry the ring Varena's giving Dill. You have to take her bouquet while she's saying her vows." Mom smiled at me, and her washed-blue eyes crinkled around the

34

corners of her eyelids. When my mother smiled, her whole face smiled with her. "You're lucky she didn't pick a dress with a ten-foot train, because you'd have to turn it around for her before she leaves the church."

I thought I could remember the ring and the bouquet.

"I'll have to thank her for the honor," I said, and Mom's face sagged for just a minute. She thought I was being sarcastic.

"I mean it," I told her, and I could almost feel her relax.

Had I been so frightening, so unpredictable, so rude?

When I'd worked my way carefully out of the dress, and pulled my T-shirt back on, I patted my mother gently on the shoulder as she made sure the dress was absolutely even on its padded hanger.

She smiled fleetingly at me, and then we went back to the kitchen to clean up.

Two

I wore the off-white blouse, gold vest, and black pants to the shower. I buttoned the blouse all the way up to the neck. My makeup was light and perfect, and my hair fluffed out in the right way. I looked fine, I decided, appropriate. I worked on relaxing, buckled into the backseat of my mother's car.

We picked up Varena on the way. This was at least her second shower, but she was as excited and pleased as though celebrating her forthcoming marriage was an original idea.

We drove across town to the home of the shower hostess, Margie Lipscom. Margie was another nurse at the little Bartley hospital, which was always threatened with closing or being closed. Margie was married to one of the more prominent lawyers in Bartley, which was actually not saying much. Bartley is a Delta town, and in this phase of its existence, that means poor.

It meant that at least seventy percent of the town's population was on welfare.

When I'd been growing up, it had just meant that Bartley was flat. You don't know what flat is until you've lived in the Delta.

I missed the low, rolling hills around Shakespeare. I missed the ratty Christmas decorations. I missed my house. I missed my gym.

I would have given anything to be selfish enough to jump in my car and drive home.

I took slow, deep breaths, like I did before I attempted to lift a weight that was a real challenge. Like I did before we sparred in karate class.

Mom drove past Bartley's dilapidated motel, and I glanced into its U of rooms. There was a car parked there—that, in itself, was nearly amazing—and it looked like . . . my heart began to stutter in an uncomfortable way.

I shook my head. Couldn't be.

We parked on the street in front of the white-painted brick house all lit up like a birthday cake. There was a white-and-silver paper wedding bell fixed to the front door. A stout redhead stood just within the foyer . . . Margie Lipscom. I'd known her as a plump brunette.

My mother got patted, my sister got hugged, and I was greeted with a shriek.

"Oh, *Lily!* Girl, you look beautiful!" Margie exclaimed. She grabbed me and embraced me. I endured it. Margie was my age, had never been a particular friend of mine; she had grown closer to my sister when they began working together. Margie had always been a hooter and a hugger. She was going to fuss extra over me now, because she felt sorry for me.

"Isn't she even prettier, Frieda?" Margie said to my mother. Overcompensating for her discomfort.

"Lily has always been lovely," my mother said calmly.

"Well, let's go see everyone!" Margie grabbed my hand and led me into the living room. I was biting the inside of my mouth. I was having a little flutter of panic and anger, the sort of nervous spasm I hadn't had in a long time. A long, long time.

I found a smile and fixed it on my face.

After I'd nodded to everyone and said, "Tell you later," in answer to almost every query, I was able to sit in a straight chair that had been crammed into a corner of the crowded living room. After that, all I had to do was aim a pleasant look in the direction of the loudest speaker, and I was fine.

This was a lingerie shower, and I'd gotten Varena a present when I'd shopped for myself in Montrose. She hadn't expected a gift from me, hadn't noticed me bring it into the house. She looked up at me in surprise when she read the card on the front. I may have imagined it, but she looked a little apprehensive.

My gift was a nightgown, full-length, with spaghetti straps and lace panels—sheer lace panels—over the breasts. It was black. It was beautiful. It was really, really sexy. As Varena was ripping off the paper, I was suddenly convinced I'd made a terrible mistake. The most daring garment Varena had received so far was a tiger-print teddy, and there had been some red faces over that.

When Varena shook out the gown and held it up, there was a moment of silence, during which I decided I might as well sneak out the back way. Then Varena said, "Wow.

This is for the wedding night." And there was a chorus of "Oooo" and "Oh, boy!"

"Lily, this is beautiful," Varena said directly. "And I bet Dill's gonna thank you, too!"

There was a chorus of laughter, and then the next gift was passed to my sister to open.

I relaxed and coasted on autopilot for the rest of the evening.

During the punch and cakes, the talk turned to Bartley's purse snatcher. This seemed an urban sort of crime for Bartley, so I paid attention. Margie was saying, "And he stole Diane's purse right off her arm and ran off with it!"

"Did she get a good look at him?" the minister's wife asked. Lou O'Shea was a buxom brunette with a ski-jump nose and intelligent eyes. I'd never met her before. I hadn't been to church, in Bartley or anywhere else, in years.

"Just a black guy, medium height," Margie said. "Could be a hundred people."

"She's all right?" my mother asked.

"Well, he knocked her down to the sidewalk, so she had some scrapes and bruises. It could've been a lot worse."

After a second's thoughtful pause, a few eyes slid in my direction. I was the worse it could have been.

But I was used to that. I kept my face blank, and the little moment passed. A purse snatching did not seem as remarkable as it would have a few years ago. Now, with gang presence and drugs in every tiny town up and down the interstate and all in between, what happened to Diane Dykeman, a sales clerk at one of the local clothing stores, didn't seem so bad. She seemed lucky to be unhurt, rather than unfortunate to have her purse snatched at all.

After a tedious two and a half hours we drove home, taking a different route this time since we were giving a lift to Lou O'Shea, whose husband had dropped her off on his way to a meeting. The Presbyterian manse was a large redbrick home that matched the adjacent church. I half listened to the backseat conversation between Varena and Lou, enough to gather that Lou, like Meredith Osborn, had an eight-year-old girl and another, younger child. When we pulled into the driveway, Lou seemed reluctant to get out.

"I'm afraid it doesn't make Krista any fonder of Luke, him crying so much," Lou told us with a heavy sigh. "She's not too enthusiastic about her little brother right now."

"Krista is Anna's age, they play together a lot," Varena reminded me.

"It'll all straighten out," my mother said in her soothing way. "Sooner or later you'll find out why Luke cries all night, and he'll stop. And then Krista will forget all about it. She's a smart little girl, Lou."

"You're right," Lou said instantly, back on her mettle as a minister's wife. "Thanks for the lift. I'll see you-all tomorrow afternoon!"

When we were driving away, Varena said, "Lou'll be coming to the rehearsal dinner tomorrow night."

"Isn't it traditional to have the rehearsal dinner the night before the wedding?" I didn't want to sound critical, but I was faintly curious.

"Yes. Dill had originally scheduled it for that night," Mother said. I was being subtly reminded that the groom's family had the responsibility for the rehearsal dinner. "But Sarah May's was already booked for the two evenings before the wedding! So we just moved it to three nights, and the couple giving the supper for Dill and Varena rescheduled it to the night before the wedding, bless them."

I nodded, hardly paying attention. I was absolutely confident I would be told what to do, when. I found myself wanting to be alone so badly I could taste it. When we got to Varena's, I unloaded the shower presents with great dispatch, and at my folks' house, I said a brief good-night to Mom before heading for my room.

My father hadn't yet gotten home from the bachelor party. I hoped he wasn't drinking and smoking cigars. His blood pressure would soar.

I sat in the little chair in my room and read for a long time, a biography I'd brought with me. Then I hooked my feet under the bed and did sit-ups, I dropped and did push-ups, and I did eighty leg lifts. After that, it was time for a relaxing shower. I noticed that my father had come in at some point and turned out the remaining lights.

But even after the hot shower, I felt itchy. I couldn't walk in Bartley. People would talk about my family. The police weren't used to me. They might stop me—if I saw any. The Bartley police force was not large.

I pushed the temptation away and forced myself to climb in the bed. I worked three crossword puzzles in a book I found in the bedside table drawer. Somehow, trying to think of a five-letter word meaning an earth-covered Indian dwelling did the trick. Finally, I was able to draw a curtain on a very long day.

Unfortunately, the next was more of the same.

Before noon, I decided that everyone in my family should have had to go to work until an hour before the wedding.

My father had taken two weeks' vacation from the electric company. Since my mother was a housewife, she was always at work—but still in the house, constantly thinking of things that just had to be done. Varena had just taken three weeks' leave from her job at the hospital, and even Dill was often leaving the drugstore to his normally part-time assistant, a young mother who was also a pharmacist.

More presents arrived, to be unwrapped and admired and entered on the list. More thank-you notes had to be written. The two other bridesmaids had to stop by and admire and check on last-minute plans. The minister, Jess O'Shea, came in for a minute to verify a couple of things. He had smooth dark blond hair and was quietly good-looking in a blocky, square-jawed way: I hoped he was as good as he was handsome, because I'd always imagined that ministers were prime targets for neurotic—or just hopeful—members of their congregation.

His little girl was in tow. Chunky Krista, whose hair was the same dark brown as her mother's but not as perfectly smooth, was sleepy-eyed and cross with her baby brother's nocturnal activity, just as Lou had predicted. Krista was in a whiny mood.

"Luke cried all night," she said sullenly when someone asked her for the third time where her brother was.

"Oh, Krista!" one of the other bridesmaids said disapprovingly. Varena's lifelong best friend, Tootsie Monahan, was blond and round-faced and low on brain cells. "How can you say that about a little kid like Luke? Toddlers are so cute."

I saw Krista's face flush. Tootsie was pushing the old guilt button hard. I'd been leaning against the wall in the living room. I shoved off and maneuvered myself closer to the little girl.

"Varena cried all night when she was baby," I told Krista very quietly.

Krista looked up at me unbelievingly. Her round hazel eyes, definitely her best feature, fastened on me with every appearance of skepticism. "Did not," she said tentatively.

"Did too." I nodded firmly and drifted into the kitchen, where I managed to sneak Krista some sort of carbonated drink that she really enjoyed. She probably wasn't supposed to have it. Then I wandered around the house, from time to time retreating to my room and shutting the door for ten minutes. (That was the length of time, I'd found from trial and error, before someone missed me and came to see how I was, what I was doing.)

Varena popped her head in my door about 12:45 to ask me if I'd go with her to the doctor's. "I need to go in to pick up my birth-control pill prescription, but I want Dr. LeMay to check my ears. The right one is feeling a little achy, and I'm scared it'll be a full-blown infection by the wedding day. Binnie said come on in, he'd see me before the afternoon patients stacked up."

One of the perks of being a nurse was the quick in-and-out you got at the local doctors' offices, Varena had told me years ago. As long as I could remember, Varena had suffered from allergies, which frequently caused ear infections. She had always developed them at the most inconvenient times. Like four days before her wedding.

I followed her out to her car with a sense of release. "I know you need to get out of the house," Varena said, giving me a little sideways glance. We pulled out of the driveway and began the short hop to Dr. LeMay's office.

"Is it that obvious?"

"Only to someone who knows you," Varena said ruefully. "Yes, Lily, it's like seeing a tiger in a cage at the zoo. Back and forth, back and forth, giving all the people who walk by that ferocious stare."

"Surely not that bad," I said anxiously. "I don't want to upset them."

"I know you don't. And I'm glad to see you caring."

"I never stopped."

"You could have fooled me."

"I just didn't have the extra . . ." Staying sane had taken all the energy I had. Trying to reassure other people had been simply impossible.

"I think I understand, finally," Varena said. "I'm sorry I brought it up. Mom and Dad know, better than me, that you care about them."

I was being forgiven for something I hadn't done, or at least had done only in Varena's opinion. But she was making an effort. I would make an effort, too.

Dr. LeMay was still based in the same little building in which he'd practiced medicine his entire career, all forty years of it. He must be nearing retirement age, his nurse Binnie Armstrong, too. They'd been a team for twenty-five years, I figured.

Varena pulled into one of the angled parking spots, and we went down the narrow sidewalk to the front door. A matching door, the one that had been labeled "Blacks Only" at the beginning of Dr. LeMay's practice, had been replaced by a picture window. In the past five years, a set of bars had been installed across the vulnerable glass. Kind of wrapped up Bartley's history in a nutshell, I decided.

The door had been painted blue to match the eaves, but the paint had already chipped to show a long-familiar shade

44

of green underneath. I twisted the knob and pushed, stepping in ahead of Varena.

The little building was oddly silent. No phones ringing, no copier running, no radio playing, no piped-in music.

I turned to look at my sister. Something was wrong. But Varena's gaze slid away from mine. She wasn't going to admit it, yet.

"Binnie!" she called too cheerfully. "Lily and I are here! Come see her." She stared at the closed door on the other side of the waiting room, the door leading back to the examining rooms and offices. The glass that enclosed the receptionist's cubicle remained empty.

We heard a faint, terrible sound. It was the sound of someone dying. I had heard it before.

I took six steps across the waiting room and opened the second door. The familiar hall, with three rooms to the right and three rooms to the left, was now floored with imitation wood-pattern linoleum instead of the speckled beige pattern I remembered, I thought incongruously.

Then I noticed the advancing rivulet of blood, the only movement in the hall. I traced it, not really wanting to find the source, but in that small space it was all too obvious. A woman in a once-white uniform lay in the doorway of the middle room on the right.

"Binnie," screamed Varena, her hands flying up to her face. But then my sister remembered that she was a nurse, and she was instantly on her knees by the bloody woman. It was hard to discern the contours of Binnie Armstrong's face and head, she was so bludgeoned. It was from her throat the noise had come.

While Varena knelt by her, trying to take her pulse, Binnie Armstrong died. I watched her whole body relax in final abandonment.

I glanced in the door to the right, the one to the receptionist's little office. Clean and empty. I looked in the room to the left, an examining room. Clean and empty. I moved carefully down the hall, while my sister did CPR on the dead nurse, and I cautiously craned around the door of the next room on the left, another examining room. Empty. The doorway Binnie lay in led to the tiny lab and storage room. I stepped carefully past my sister and found Dr. LeMay in the last room to the right, his office.

"Varena," I said sharply.

Varena looked up, dabbled with blood from the corpse.

"Binnie's dead, Varena." I nodded in the direction of the office. "Come check Dr. LeMay."

Varena leaped to her feet and took a couple of steps to stare in the door. Then she was moving to the other side of the desk to take his pulse but shaking her head as she went.

"He was killed at his desk," she said, as though that made it worse.

Dr. LeMay's white hair was clotted with blood. It was pooled on the desk where his head lay. His glasses were askew, ugly black-framed trifocals, and I wanted so badly to set them square on his face—as if, when I did, he would see again. I had known Dr. LeMay my whole life. He had delivered me.

Varena touched his hand, which was resting on the desk. I noticed in a stunned, slow way that it was absolutely clean. He had not had a chance to fight back. The first blow had been a devastating one. The room was full of paper, files and claim forms and team physicals . . . most of it now spotted with blood.

"He's gone," Varena whispered, not that there had been any doubt.

"We need to get out of here," I said, my voice loud and sharp in the little room with its awful sights and smells.

And we stared at each other, our eyes widening with a sudden shared terror.

I jerked my head toward the front door, and Varena scooted past me. She ran out while I waited to see if anything moved.

I was the only live person in the office.

I followed Varena out.

She was already across the street at the State Farm Insurance office, pulling open the glass door and lifting the receiver off the phone on the receptionist's desk. That stout and permed lady, wearing a bright red blouse and a Christmas corsage, was looking up at Varena as if she were speaking Navaho into the telephone. Within two minutes a police car pulled up in front of Dr. LeMay's office, and a tall, thin black man got out.

"You the one called in?" he asked.

"My sister, in the office over there." I nodded toward the plate-glass window, through which Varena could be seen sitting in the client's chair, sobbing. The woman with the corsage was bending over her, offering Varena some tissues.

"I'm Detective Brainerd," the man said reassuringly, as though I'd indicated I'd thought he might be an imposter. "Did you go in the building here?"

"Yes."

"Did you see Dr. LeMay and his nurse?"

"Yes."

"And they're dead."

"Yes."

"Is there anyone else in the building?"

"No."

"So, is there a gas leak, or was there a fire smoldering, maybe smoke inhalation . . . ?"

"They were both beaten." My gaze skimmed the top of the old, old gum trees lining the street. "To death."

"Okay, now. I'll tell you what we're going to do here."

He was extremely nervous, and I didn't blame him one bit.

"You're gonna stay right here, ma'am, while I go in there and take a look. Don't go anywhere, now."

"No."

I waited by the police car, the cold gray day pinching my face and hands.

This is a world of carnage and cruelty: I had momentarily put that aside in the false security of my hometown, in the optimistic atmosphere of my sister's marriage.

I began to detach from the scene, to float away, escaping this town, this building, these dead. It had been a long time since I'd retreated like this, gone to the remote place where I was not responsible for feeling.

A young woman was standing in front of me in a paramedic's uniform.

"Ma'am? Ma'am? Are you all right?" Her dark, anxious face peered into mine, her black hair stiff, smooth, and shoulder length under a cap with a caduceus patch on it.

"Yes."

"Officer Brainerd said you had seen the bodies."

I nodded.

"Are you . . . maybe you better come sit down over here, ma'am."

My eyes followed her pointing finger to the rear of the ambulance.

"No, thanks," I said politely. "My sister is over there in the State Farm office, though. She might need help."

"I think you may need a little help yourself, ma'am," the woman said earnestly, loudly, as though I was retarded, as though I couldn't tell the difference between clinical shock and just being numb.

"No." I said it as finally and definitely as I knew how. I waited. I heard her muttering to someone else, but she did leave me alone after that. Varena came to stand beside me. Her eyes were red, and her makeup was streaked.

"Let's go home," she said.

"The policeman told me to wait."

"Oh."

Just then the same policeman, Brainerd, came striding out of the doctor's office. He'd gotten over his fit of nerves, and he'd seen the worst. He was focused, ready to go to work. He asked us a lot of questions, keeping us out in the cold for half an hour when we'd told him the sum of our knowledge in one minute.

Finally, we buckled up in Varena's car. As she started back to our parents' house, I switched Varena's heater to full blast. I glanced over at my sister. Her face was blanched by the cold, her eyes red from crying with her contacts in. She'd pulled her hair back this morning in a ponytail, with a bright red scarf tied over the elastic band. The scarf still looked crisp and cheerful, though Varena had wilted. Varena's eyes met mine while we were waiting our turn at a four-way stop. She said, "The drug cabinet was closed and full."

"I saw." Dr. LeMay had always kept the samples, and his

supplies, in the same cabinet in the lab, a glass-front old-fashioned one. Since I'd been his patient as a child, that cabinet had stood in the same place with the same sort of contents. It would have surprised me profoundly if Dr. LeMay had ever kept anything very street-desirable . . . he'd have antibiotics, antihistamines, skin ointments, that kind of thing, I thought vaguely. Maybe painkillers.

Like Varena, I'd seen past Binnie's body that the cabinet door was shut and everything in the room was orderly. It didn't seem likely that the same person who would commit such messy murders would leave the drug cabinet so neat if he'd searched it.

"I don't know what to make of that," I told Varena. She shook her head. She didn't, either. I stared out of the window at the familiar passing scenery, wishing I was anywhere but in Bartley.

"Lily, are you all right?" Varena asked, her voice curiously hesitant.

"Sure, are you?" I sounded more abrupt than I'd intended.

"I have to be, don't I? The wedding rehearsal is tonight, and I don't see how we can call it off. Plus, I've seen worse, frankly. It's just it being Dr. LeMay and Binnie that gave me such a wallop."

My sister sounded simply matter-of-fact. It hit me forcefully that Varena, as a nurse, had seen more blood and pain and awfulness than I would see in a lifetime. She was practical. After overcoming the initial shock, she was tough. She pulled into our parents' driveway and switched off the ignition.

"You're right. You can't call it off. People die all the time, Varena, and you can't derail your wedding because of it."

We were just the Practical Sisters.

"Right," she said, looking at me oddly. "We have to go in and tell Mom and Dad."

I stared at the house in front of us as if I had never seen it. "Yes. Let's go."

But it was Varena who got out of the car first. And it was Varena who told my parents the bad news, in a grave, firm voice that somehow implied that any emotional display would be in bad taste.

THREE

The rehearsal was scheduled for six o'clock, and we arrived at the Presbyterian church on the dot. Tootsie Monahan was already there, her hair in long curly strands like a show poodle's, talking and laughing with Dill and his best man. It was apparent that no one was going to talk about the death of the doctor and his nurse, unless they went into a corner and whispered. Everyone was struggling to keep this a joyous occasion, or at the very least to hold the emotional level above grim.

I was introduced to Berry Duff, Dill's former college roommate and present best man, with some significance. After all, we were both single and in the same age group. The barely unspoken hope was that something might happen.

Berry Duff was very tall, with thinning dark hair, wide dark eyes, and an enviable olive complexion. He was a farmer in Mississippi, had been divorced for about three years, and, I was given to understand, the embodiment of all things desirable: well-to-do, solid, religious, divorced without child custody. Dill managed to cram a surprising amount of that information into his introduction, and after a few minutes' conversation with Berry, I learned the rest.

Berry seemed like a nice guy, and it was pleasant to stand with him while we waited for the players to assemble. I was not much of a person for small talk, and Berry didn't seem to mind, which was refreshing. He took his time poking around conversationally for some common ground, found it in dislike of movie theaters and love of weight lifting, which he'd enjoyed in college.

I was wearing the white dress with the black jacket. At the last minute my mother had insisted I needed some color besides my lipstick, a point I was willing to concede. She'd put a filmy scarf in autumn reds and golds around my neck and anchored it with the gold pin I'd brought.

"You look very nice," Dill said, on one of his pass-bys. He and Varena seemed to be awfully nervous and were inventing errands to send them pacing around the small church. We were all hovering near the front, since the back was in darkness beyond the last pew. The door close to the pulpit, opening into a hall leading past the minister's study, gave a pneumatic hiss as people came and went. The heavier door beyond the big open area at the back of the church thudded from time to time as the members of the wedding party assembled.

Finally, everyone was there. Varena; Tootsie; me; the other bridesmaid, Janna Russell; my mother and father; Jess and Lou O'Shea, the one in his capacity as minister and the other in her capacity as church organist; Dill; Berry Duff;

Dill's unmarried younger brother Jay; a cousin of Dill's, Matthew Kingery; the florist who'd been hired to supply the wedding flowers, who would double as wedding director; and miracle of miracles, Dill's mother, Lula. Watching the relief spread over Varena's face as the old woman stomped in on Jay's arm made me want to take Lula Kingery aside and have a few sharp words with her.

I watched the woman closely while the florist was giving the assembled group some directions. It didn't take long to conclude that Dill's mother was a few bricks short of a load. She was inappropriately dressed (a short-sleeved floral housedress with a hole in it, high heels with rhinestone buckles), which was in itself no clear signal of mental derangement, but when you added the ensemble to her out-of-the-ballpark questions ("Do I have to walk down the aisle too?") and her constant hand and eye movement, the sum total was significant.

Well. So Dill's family had a skeleton, too.

Notch one up for my family. At least I could pretty much be relied on to do the right thing, if I actually made an appearance. Dill's mom was definitely a loose cannon.

Varena was handling Mrs. Kingery with amazing tact and kindness. So were my parents. I felt a proprietary swell of pride at my folks' goodness and had to resume my conversation with Berry Duff to cover the rush of emotion.

After even more last-minute toing and froing, the rehearsal began. Patsy Green, the florist, gathered us together and gave us our marching orders. We took our positions to walk through the ceremonial paces.

Getting the cues straight from Lou O'Shea on the organ, an usher escorted Mrs. Kingery to her place at the front of the church. Then my mother was guided to her front pew on the other side.

While I clustered with the other bridesmaids at the back of the church, Jess O'Shea came in from the hall that ran in front of his office to the church sanctuary. He went to the top of the steps in front of the altar and stood there smiling. Dill entered the sanctuary from the same door, accompanied by Berry, who grinned at me. Then I walked down the aisle, listening with one ear to the florist's adjuration to walk slowly and smoothly.

I always walk smoothly.

She reminded me to smile.

Jay Kingery came in from the hall, and Janna started down the aisle. Then the groomsman, cousin Matthew, took his place, and Tootsie did her long walk. I set off on cue, with Patsy Green hissing "Smile!" at my back.

Then the pièce de résistance. Varena came down the aisle on my father's arm, and she looked flushed and happy. So did Dad. Dill was beaming like a fool at his bride. Berry raised an eyebrow at me, and I felt my mouth twitch in response.

"That went well!" Patsy Green called from the back of the church. She began walking toward us, and we all turned to listen to her comments. I wasn't at all surprised it had fallen into place, since almost everyone in the party was old enough to have played a role in a score of weddings and been a major participant in a daunting number.

My attention drifted, and I began looking around the church, the one I'd attended every Sunday as a child. The walls always seemed newly painted a brilliant white, and the carpet was always replaced with same deep green as the cushions on the pews. The high ceiling always made me think *up*—space, infinity, the omnipotent unknown.

I heard a little cough and brought my gaze down from the infinite to stare into the pews. Someone was in the shadows at the back of the church. My heart started pounding in an uncomfortable way. Before I had formed a thought, I began to walk down the steps and the long strip of green carpet. I didn't even feel my feet moving.

He stood up and moved to the door.

At the moment I reached him, he opened the door for me, and we stepped out into the cold night. In one move, he pulled me to him and kissed me.

"Jack," I said when I could breathe, "Jack."

My hands went under his suit coat to touch his back through his striped shirt.

He kissed me again. His hands tightened on me, pressed me harder against his body.

"Glad to see me," I observed after a while. My breathing was not even.

"Yeah," he said hoarsely.

I pulled away a little to look at him. "You're wearing a tie."

"I knew you'd be dressed up. I had to look as nice as you."

"You a psychic detective?"

"Just a damn good one."

"Umhum. What are you doing in Bartley?"

"You don't think I'm here just to see you?"

"No."

"You're almost wrong."

"Almost?" I felt a mixture of relief and disappointment.

"Yes, ma'am. Last week, I was clearing off my desk so I could come down here to lend you some moral support—or maybe morale support—when I got a call from an old friend of mine."

"And?"

"Can I tell you later? Say, at my motel room?"

"That *was* your car I saw! How long have you been here?" For a moment I wondered if Jack had revealed his presence just because he'd figured I'd identify his car sooner or later, in a town the size of Bartley.

"Since yesterday. Later? God, you look good," he said, and his mouth traveled down my neck. His fingers pulled the scarf away from my neck. Despite the cold, I began to have that warmth that meant I was just as glad to see him, especially after the horrors of the day.

"OK, I'll come by to hear your story, but it'll have to be after the rehearsal dinner," I said firmly. I gasped a second later. "No, Jack. This is my sister's wedding. This is a have-to."

"I admire a woman who sticks to her principles." His voice was low and rough.

"Will you come in and meet my family?"

"That's why I'm wearing the suit."

I looked up at him with some suspicion. Jack is a little older than I am and four inches taller. In the security lights of the church parking lot, I could see that he had his black hair brushed back into a neat ponytail, as usual. He has a beautiful thin, prominent nose, and his lips are thin and sculpted. Jack used to be a Memphis policeman, until he left the force after his involvement in an unsavory and bloody scandal.

He's got lips, he knows how to use 'em, I thought, almost intoxicated by his presence. Only Jack could get me in the mood to paraphrase an old ZZ Top song.

"Let's go do the right thing, before I try something here in the parking lot," he suggested.

I stared at him and turned to walk back in the church. Somehow, I expected him to vanish between the door and the altar, but he followed me in and down the aisle, flanking me when we reached the clustered wedding party. Naturally enough, they were all staring our way. I could feel my face harden. I hate explaining myself.

And Jack stepped up beside me, put his arm around me, and said, "You must be Lily's mother! I'm Jack Leeds, Lily's . . ."

I waited with some interest while Jack, normally a smooth talker, floundered at the end of the sentence.

"Boyfriend," he finished, with a certain inaccuracy.

"Frieda Bard," my mother said, looking a little stunned. "This is my husband, Gerald."

"Mr. Bard," Jack said respectfully, "glad to meet you."

My father pumped Jack's hand, beaming like someone who's just found Ed McMahon and a camera crew on his doorstep. Even the ponytail and the scar on Jack's right cheek didn't diminish my father's smile. Jack's suit was expensive, a very muted brown plaid that brought out the color of his hazel eyes. His shoes were polished. He looked prosperous, healthy, clean shaven, and I looked happy. That was enough for my dad, at least for the moment.

"And you must be Varena." Jack turned to my sister.

When would everyone stop looking like deer caught in headlights? You'd think I was a damn leper, they were so amazed I had a man. Jack actually kissed Varena, a quick light one on the forehead. "Kiss the bride for luck," he said, with that sudden, brilliant smile that was so winning.

Dill recovered quickest.

"I'm about to join the family," he told Jack. "I'm Dill Kingery."

"Pleased to meet you." The shake again.

And it went on from there, with me not saying a word. Jack glad-handed the men and gave the women a flash of clean, earnest sexuality. Even off-kilter Mrs. Kingery beamed at him in a dazed way. "You're trouble on the hoof, and I know it," she said firmly.

Everyone froze in horror, but Jack laughed with genuine amusement. The moment passed, and I saw Dill close his eyes in relief.

"I'll take off, since you're in the middle of your special occasion," Jack told the group generally, with no hint of a hint in his voice. "I just wanted to meet Lily's folks."

"Please," Dill said instantly, "we'd really enjoy your joining us for the rehearsal dinner."

Jack did the polite thing and declined, mentioning the important family occasion and the fact that he had arrived unannounced.

Dill repeated his invitation. Social Ping-Pong.

When Varena joined in, Jack allowed himself to be persuaded.

He retired to sit at the back of the church. My eyes followed him every inch of the way.

We walked through the ceremony again. I went through my paces on autopilot. Patsy Green reminded me again to smile. This time she sounded a little sharper.

I was thinking hard during the rest of the rehearsal, but I couldn't come to any conclusion. Could it possibly be true that Jack was here for me? He had admitted he had another reason, but he'd said he was coming here anyway. If that was true . . .

But it was too painful to believe.

Jack had already been here when Dr. LeMay and Binnie Armstrong were done to death. So his arrival couldn't be connected with the double murder.

"Looks like I'm too late on the scene," Berry said to me in a pleasant way after Patsy Green and the O'Sheas agreed we had the procedure down pat. We were just outside the church doors.

"That's so flattering of you," I said with a genuine smile. For once, I had said the right thing. He smiled back at me.

"Lily!" Jack called. He was holding open the passenger door of his car. I couldn't imagine why.

"Excuse me," I told Berry and strolled over. "Since when," I muttered, conscious of my voice carrying in the cold clear air, "have you found it necessary to hold doors for me?"

Jack looked wounded. "Darlin', I'm your slave." He seemed to be imitating Berry's Delta accent.

"Don't be an ass," I whispered. "Seeing you is so good. Don't ruin it."

He stared down at me as I swung my legs into his car. The taut muscles around his mouth relaxed. "All right," he said and shut the door.

We backed up to follow the other cars out of the parking lot.

"You found the doctor today," he said.

"Yes. How did you know?"

"I brought my police scanner. Are you OK?"

"Yes."

"How much do you know about Dill Kingery?" he asked.

I felt as though he'd punched me in the stomach. I had to sit silent to gather breath, my panic was so complete and sudden. "Is something wrong with him?" I asked finally, my voice coming out not so much angry as scared. Varena's face smiling up at Dill came into my mind, the long engagement, the relationship Varena had worked so hard to build up with Dill's daughter, Varena's cheerful acceptance of crazy Mrs. Kingery . . .

"Probably nothing. Just tell me."

"He's a pharmacist. He's a widower. He's a father. He pays his bills on time. His mother is crazy."

"That's the old biddy who said I was trouble?"

"Yes." She was right.

"The first wife's been dead how long?"

"Six or seven years. Anna doesn't remember her."

"And Jess O'Shea? The preacher?"

I looked over at Jack as we passed a streetlight. His expression was tense, almost angry. That made two of us. "I don't know anything about him. I've met his wife and little girl. They have a boy, too."

"He coming to the rehearsal dinner?"

"The minister usually does. Yes, I heard them say they'd gotten a sitter."

I wanted to hit Jack, a not uncommon situation.

We pulled into Sarah May's Restaurant parking lot. Jack parked a little away from the other cars.

"I can't believe you've upset me this much in five minutes," I said, hearing my own voice coming out distant and cold. And shaking.

He stared through the windshield at the restaurant windows. They were edged with flickering Christmas lights. The glow flashed across his face. *Damn* blinking lights. After what felt like a very long time, Jack turned to me. He took my left hand with his right.

"Lily, when I explain what I'm working on, you'll forgive me," he said, with a kind of painful sincerity I was forced to respect. He sat holding my hand, making no move to open his door, waiting for me to extend him . . . trust? Advance absolution? I felt as if he'd opened a cavity in my chest and turned a spotlight on it.

I nodded sharply, opened my door, and got out. We met in front of the car. He took my hand again, and we went into Sarah May's.

Sarah Cawthorne, half of the Sarah May of the name, showed us to the private room that Dill had reserved for the party. Of course, all of us but Jack and Mrs. Kingery had been in it many times, since it was one of two places in Bartley you could dine out privately. I saw that it had been recently carpeted and wallpapered in the apparently perpetually popular hunter green and burgundy, and the artificial Christmas tree in the corner had been decorated with burgundy and off-white lace and matching ribbons. This tree was lit, too, of course, draped with the small clear lights, and thank God they didn't blink.

The tables had Christmas centerpieces in the same colors, and the place mats were cloth and so were the napkins. (This was very swank for Bartley.) The U-shaped banquet arrangement hadn't changed, though, and as we all drifted to our seats I realized that Jack was maneuvering us toward the O'Sheas. He was steering me unobtrusively with his hand on my back, and I was reminded of a puppet sitting on a ventriloquist's knee, the controlling hand hidden in a hole in the puppet's back. Jack caught my look, and his hand dropped away.

Dill was already standing behind a chair with my sister on one side and his mother on the other, so only Jess O'Shea was available as a target.

Jack managed to slot us between the O'Sheas. I was between the two men, and to Jack's right was Lou. Across the table from us was Patsy Green, squired by one of the ushers, a banker who played golf with Dill, I remembered.

The salads were served almost immediately, and Dill properly asked Jess to say grace. Of course, Jess obliged. Next to me, Jack bowed his head and shut his eyes, but his hand found mine and his fingers wrapped tightly around mine. He brought my hand to his mouth and kissed it—I could feel his warm lips, the hint of teeth—then deposited the hand back in my lap and relaxed his grip. When Jess said, "Amen," Jack let go and spread his napkin on his lap as though the little moment had been a dream.

I glanced up and down the table to see if anyone had noticed, and the only eyes that met mine were my mother's. She looked as though she were half embarrassed by the sexuality of the gesture . . . but pleased by the emotional wallop of it.

I had no idea what my own face looked like. A salad was placed in front of me, and I stared down blindly at it. When the waitress asked me what dressing I wanted, I answered her at random, and she dolloped my lettuce and tomato with a bright orange substance.

Jack began gently questioning Lou about her life. He was so good at it that few civilians would have suspected he had a hidden agenda. I tried not to speculate on the nature of that agenda.

I turned to Jess, who was having a little trouble with a jar of bacon bits. After the nicely decorated room, plunking the jar of bits down on the table reminded me firmly we were in Bartley. I held out my hand with a give-me curve of the fingers.

Somewhat surprised, Jess handed me the jar. I gripped it firmly, inhaled. I twisted as I exhaled. The lid came off. I handed the jar to him.

When I looked up in his face, there was a kind of dubious amusement on it.

Dubious was OK. Amusement wasn't.

"You're very strong," he observed.

"Yes," I said. I took a bite of salad, then remembered that Jack needed to know more about this man.

"Did you grow up in a town bigger than Bartley?" I asked.

"Oh, not bigger at all," he said genially. "Ocolona, Mississippi. My folks still live there."

"And your wife, is she from Mississippi also?"

I hated this.

"Yes, but from Pass Christian. We met in college at Ole Miss."

"And then you went to seminary?"

"Yes, four years at Westminster Theological Seminary in Philadelphia. Lou and I just had to put our trust in the Lord. It was a long separation. In fact, after the first two years, I missed being away from her so much, we got married. She held any job she could get in the area while I worked to graduate. She played the organ at churches, she played the piano for parties. She even worked at a fast-food place, God bless her." Jess's square, handsome face relaxed and warmed as he talked about his wife. I felt acutely uncomfortable.

The salad dressing was thick as sour cream, and sweet. I shoved the most heavily laden lettuce to one side and tried to eat the rest. I couldn't just sit there and question him.

"And you," he began the conversational return, "what's your occupation?"

Someone who didn't know my life history?

"I'm a house cleaner, and I run errands for people. I decorate Christmas trees for businesses. I take old ladies grocery shopping."

"A girl Friday, though I guess 'girl' is politically incorrect now." He gave the strained smile of a conservative paying lip service to liberality.

"Yes," I said.

"And you live in Arkansas?"

"Yes." I prodded myself mentally. "Shakespeare."

"Any bigger than Bartley?"

"Yes."

He eyed me with a determined smile. "And have you lived there long?"

"Over four years now. I bought a house." There, that was contributing to the conversation. What did Jack want to know about this man?

"What do you do in your spare time?"

"I work out. Lifting weights. And I take karate." And now I see Jack. The thought sent a warm rush through my pelvis. I remembered his lips against my hand.

"And your friend Mr. Leeds? Does he live in Shake-speare?"

"No, Jack lives in Little Rock."

"He works there, too?"

Did Jack want it known what he did?

"His job takes him different places," I said neutrally. "Did Lou have Luke—isn't that your little boy's name?— here in the Shakespeare hospital?" People really like to talk about their childbirth experiences.

"Yes, right here at the hospital. We were a little worried . . . there are some emergencies this hospital can't handle. But Lou is healthy, and indications were that the baby was healthy, so we decided it would be better to show our faith in the local people. And it was just a great experience."

Lucky for you and Luke and Lou, I thought. "And Krista?" I asked, thinking this meal would never end. We hadn't even gotten our entrees. "Did you have her here? No, she's at least eight, and you've been here only three years, I believe?"

"Right. No, we moved here from Philadelphia with Krista." But something about the way he said it was odd.

"She was born at one of the big hospitals there? That must have been a very different experience from having your little boy here."

He said, "Are you older than Varena?"

Whoa. Change of subject. And a clumsy one. Anyone could tell I was older than Varena.

"Yes."

"You must have traveled around some in your life, too," the minister observed. The strip lights above the table winked off his blond hair, about ten shades darker than mine and certainly more natural. "You've been in Shakespeare for

66

about four years . . . did you ever live here, in Bartley, after you got out of college?"

"I lived in Memphis after I graduated from college," I said, knowing that would probably cue his memory. Someone had to have told him the story, since he'd been living here more than three years. My history was part of town folklore, just like Mrs. Fontenot shooting her equally married lover on the courthouse lawn in 1931.

"Memphis," he repeated, suddenly looking a little uneasy.

"Yes, I worked for a big housecleaning service there as a scheduler and supervisor," I said deliberately.

That flipped his memory switch. I saw his pleasant, bland face grow rigid, trying to restrain his dismay at his faux pas.

"Of course, that was years ago, now," I said, easing him off the horns of the dilemma.

"Yes, a long time," he said. He looked sorry for me for a minute, then said tactfully, "I haven't had a chance to ask Dill where he and Varena plan to go on their honeymoon."

I nodded dismissively and turned to Jack just at the instant he turned to me. Our eyes met, and he smiled that smile that altered his whole face, deep arcs appearing from his nose to his lips. Instead of the tough reserve of his defense-against-the-world face, he looked infectiously happy.

I leaned over so my lips almost touched his ear. "I have an early Christmas present for you," I said very softly.

His eyes flared wide in surmise.

"You'll like it very much," I promised, breathing the words.

During the rest of the meal, whenever Jack wasn't engaged in talking to Lou O'Shea or charming my mother, he was giving me little glances full of speculation.

We left soon after the dessert plates were cleared away. Jack seemed torn between talking to Dill and Varena and rushing me back to his hotel. I made it as difficult for him as I possibly could. As we stood making conversation with Dill, I held his hand and made circles on his palm with my thumb, very gently, very lightly.

After a few seconds, he dropped my hand to grip my arm almost painfully.

"Good-bye, Frieda, Gerald," he said to my parents, after he'd thanked Dill for inviting him. My mother and father beamed happily at him. "I'll be bringing Lily home later. We have some catching up to do."

I could see my father's mouth open to ask where this "catching up" would take place, and I saw my mother's elbow connect with his ribs, a gentle reminder to my father that I was nearly thirty-two. So Dad kept his smile in place, but it was weaker.

Waving at everyone, smiling hard, we got out the door and hurried through the freezing air to scramble into Jack's car. We had scarcely shut the doors when Jack put his fingers under my chin and turned my face to his. His mouth covered mine in a long, breathless kiss. His hands began reacquainting themselves with my topography.

"The others'll be coming out in a minute," I reminded him.

Jack said something really vile and turned on his engine. We drove to the motel in silence, Jack keeping both hands on the wheel and his eyes straight ahead.

"This place is horrible," he warned me, unlocking the

door and pushing it open. He reached in past me to switch on a light.

I pulled the drapes shut all the way and turned to him, sliding out of my black jacket as I turned. He was wrapped around me before I had my arm out of the second sleeve. We undressed in stages, interrupted by the long making out that Jack loved. He was fumbling in his suitcase with one hand for those little square foil packages, when I said, "Christmas present."

He raised his eyebrows.

"I got an implant. You don't have to use anything."

"Oh, Lily," he breathed, closing his eyes to savor the moment. He looked like a Boy Scout who'd just been given the ingredients for S'mores. I wondered when he would work out the other implications of my gift. Then Jack slid on top of me, and I quit caring.

We were wrapped in the bed together an hour later, having finally pulled down the spread and the blanket and the sheets. The sheets, at least, looked clean. One of Jack's legs was thrown across mine, securing me.

"Why are you here?" I asked. This was when Jack liked to talk.

"Lily," he said slowly, taking pleasure in saying it. "I was going to come to see you here. I did think you might need me, or at least that seeing me might help." One long finger traced my spine as I lay facing him, my face tucked in the hollow of his neck. To my horror, I could feel my nose clog up and my eyes fill. I kept my face turned down. A tear trickled down my cheek, and since I was on my side it ran into the curve of one nostril and then underneath. So elegant.

"And then Roy called me. You remember Roy?"

I nodded, so he could feel my head move.

I recalled Roy Costimiglia as a short, stout man with thinning gray hair, probably in his late fifties. You could pass him six times on the street and never remember you'd seen him before. Roy was the detective with whom Jack had served his two-year apprenticeship.

"Roy and I had talked over supper one night when Roy's wife was out of town, so he knew I was seeing a woman who had originally come from Bartley. He called because he'd been given one more lead to run down in a case he's had for four years."

I surreptitiously wiped my face with a bit of sheet.

"What case is that?" My voice did not sound too wobbly.

"Summer Dawn Macklesby." Jack's voice was as bleak and grim as I'd ever heard it. "You remember the baby girl who was kidnapped?"

And I felt cold all over again.

"I read just a little of the update story in the paper."

"So did a lot of people, and one of them reacted pretty strangely. The last paragraph of the article mentioned that Roy has been working for the Macklesby family for the past few years. Through Roy, the Macklesbys have run down every lead, checked every piece of information, every rumor, that's come to them for the past four and a half years . . . ever since they felt the police had more or less given up on the case. The Macklesbys hoped there would be some response to the story, and that's why they consented to do it. They're really nice people. I've met them. Of course, they've kind of disintegrated since she's been gone . . . the baby."

Jack kissed my cheek, and his arms tightened around me. He knew I had been crying. He was not going to talk about it.

"What response was there to the story? A phone call?"

"This." Jack sat up on the side of the bed. He unlocked his briefcase and pulled out two pieces of paper. The first was a copy of the same article I'd seen in the newspaper, with the sad picture of the Macklesbys now and the old picture of the baby in her infant seat. The Macklesbys looked as though something had chewed them up and spit them out: Teresa Macklesby, especially, was haggard with eyes that had seen hell. Her husband, Simon's, face was almost taut with restraint, and the hand that rested on his knee was clenched in a fist.

The second piece of paper was a picture from the local elementary school memory book, last year's edition; *"The Bartley Banner"* was printed, with the date, across the top of the page, page 23. The picture at the top of the page, below the heading, was an enlarged black-and-white snapshot of three little girls playing on a slide. The one flying down, her long hair trailing behind her, was Eve Osborn. The girl waiting her turn at the top of the slide was Krista O'Shea, looking much happier than I'd seen her. The child climbing the ladder had turned to smile at the camera, and my breath caught in my throat.

The caption read, "These second graders enjoy the new playground equipment donated in March by Bartley Tractor and Tire Company and Choctaw County Welding."

"This was paper-clipped to the article from the paper," Jack said. "It was in a mailing envelope postmarked Bartley. Someone here in town thinks one of these little girls is Summer Dawn Macklesby."

"Oh, no."

His finger brushed the third child's face. "Dill's girl? Anna Kingery?"

I nodded, covered my own face with my hands.

"Sweetheart, I have to do this."

"Why did you come instead of Roy?"

"Because Roy had a heart attack two days ago. He called me from his hospital bed."

FOUR

Is he going to be OK?"

"I don't know," Jack said. He was sad, and angry, too, though I wasn't sure where the anger came in. Maybe his own helplessness. "All those years of eating wrong and not exercising . . . but the main thing is, he just has a bad heart."

I sat up, too, and put my arms around Jack. For a moment he accepted the comfort. He rested his head on my shoulder, his arms encircling me. I'd taken the band off his ponytail, and his long black hair fell soft against my skin. But then he raised his head and looked at me, our faces inches apart.

"I have to do this, Lily. For Roy. He took me in and trained me. If it was anyone but him, any case but one involving a child, I'd turn it down since it concerns someone close to you . . . but this I have to do." Even if Anna Kingery turned out to be Summer Dawn Macklesby, even if Varena's life was ruined. I looked back at him, the pain in my heart so complicated I could not think how to express it.

"If he did that," Jack said, so intent on me he had read my silent thoughts, "you couldn't let her marry him anyway."

I nodded, still trying to accommodate this sharp pang. For all the years we'd spent apart, for all our estrangement, Varena was my sister, and we were the only people in the world who shared, who would remember, our common family life.

"This has to be resolved before the wedding," I said.

"Two days? Three?"

I actually had to think. "Three."

"Shit," Jack said.

"What do you have?" I pulled away from him, and his head began to lower to my breasts, as if drawn by a magnet. I grabbed his ears. "Jack, we have to finish talking."

"Then you'll have to cover up." He got his bathrobe out of the tiny closet and tossed it to me. It was the one he carried when he traveled, a thin, red, silky one, and I belted it around me.

"That's not much better," he said after a thorough look. "But it'll have to do." He pulled on a T-shirt and some Jockeys. He set his briefcase on the bed, and because it was cold in that bleak motel room, we both crawled back under the covers, sitting with our backs propped against the wall.

Jack put on his reading glasses, little half-lens ones that made him even sexier. I didn't know how long he'd used them, but he'd only recently begun wearing them in front of me. This was the first time I hadn't appreciated the effect.

"First, to find out who the little girls were, Roy hired Aunt Betty."

"Who?"

74

"You haven't met Aunt Betty yet. She's another PI, lives in Little Rock. She's amazing. In her fifties, hair dyed a medium brown, looks respectable to the core. She looks like everybody's Aunt Betty. Her real name is Elizabeth Fry. People tell her the most amazing things, because she looks like . . . well, their aunt! And damn, that woman can listen!"

"Why'd Roy send her instead of you?"

"Well, surprise, but in some situations I don't blend in like Aunt Betty does. I was good for the Shakespeare job since I look just like someone who'd work in a sporting goods store, but I don't look like I could go around a small town asking for the names of little girls and get away with it. Right?"

I tried not to laugh. That was certainly true.

"So that's the kind of job Aunt Betty's perfect for. She found out who prints the most school memory books in the state, went to them, told them she was from a private school and she was looking for a printer. The guy gave her all kinds of samples to show her parents committee."

Jack seemed to want me to acknowledge Aunt Betty's cleverness, so I nodded.

"Then," he continued, "Betty comes down to Bartley, goes in to see the elementary school principal, shows her all the samples of memory books she has, and tells the principal she works for a printing company that can give them a competitive bid on the next memory book."

"And?"

"Then she asks to see this year's Bartley memory book, notices the slide picture, asks the principal who the photographer was, maybe her company might be able to use him for extra work. Betty figured the shot was good enough to justify the lie."

I shook my head. Betty must be persuasive and totally respectable and nonthreatening. I'd known the elementary school principal, Beryl Trotter, for fifteen years, and she was not a fool.

"How does it help, having the whole book?" I asked.

"If worst had come to worst, we would have looked at all the faces in the class section until we had them matched, so we could get their names. Or Betty would have called on the man who took the picture and coasted the conversation along until he told her who the girls were. But, as it happened, Mrs. Trotter asked Betty to have a cup of coffee, and Betty found out everything from Mrs. Trotter."

"The names of the girls? Their parents? Everything?"

"Yep."

This was a little frightening.

"So, once we had the names of the parents, we were able to do some background on the O'Sheas, since he's a minister and they have several professional directories that give little biographies. Dill, too, because the pharmacists have a state association. Chock full of information. The Osborns were harder. Aunt Betty had to go to Makepeace Furniture, pretend she'd just moved in and was shopping for a new table. It was risky. But she managed to talk to Emory, find out a few things about him, and get out without having to give a local address or mention any local relatives whom he could check up on."

"So then you knew the names of the girls and their parents, and some facts about their parents."

"Yep. Then we got busy on the computers, and then I started traveling."

I felt overwhelmed. I'd never talked to Jack in any depth about what he did. I'd never fully realized that one of the qualifications for a successful private detective is the ability to lie convincingly and at the drop of a hat. I pulled away from Jack a little. He took some papers from his briefcase.

"This is a computer-enhanced drawing of Summer Dawn as she may look now," he said, apparently not conscious of my unhappiness. "Of course, we have photographs of her only as an infant. Who knows how accurate this is?"

I looked at the picture. It looked like someone, all right, but it could have been any of the girls. I decided that the drawing looked most like Krista O'Shea, because it depicted Summer Dawn still plump-cheeked, like the baby snapshot the newspaper had printed.

"I thought these were supposed to be really accurate," I said. "Does it look so anonymous because she was a baby when she vanished?"

"Partly. And as it happens, none of the pictures of Summer Dawn was really good to use for this. The Macklesbys took fewer pictures of her than of their other two children because Summer Dawn was the third child, and the third child just doesn't get photographed as much as number one and number two. The picture that appeared in the newspaper was really the best one the parents had. They had an appointment to get Summer's picture made the week she disappeared."

I didn't want to think about that. I shuffled the top drawing, looked at the other three. The second was of the same face but framed by long, straight hair. In the third, a somewhat thinner-cheeked version of Summer Dawn was topped with short, wavy hair. There was a fourth, with medium-length hair and glasses.

"One of her sisters is nearsighted," Jack explained.
Eight years.

"She has sisters?" I kept my voice level. At least I tried.

"Yeah. Two. They're fourteen and sixteen, now. Teenagers, with posters on their walls of musicians I've never listened to. Closets full of clothes. Boyfriends. And a little sister they don't remember at all."

"The Macklesbys must have money." Hiring a private detective for all those years would be expensive, and paying for the extra services of Aunt Betty and Jack.

"They're well-off. Simon Macklesby reacted to the kidnapping by throwing himself into his work. He's a partner in an office supplies business that's taken off since offices became computerized. No matter how much money they've got, the Macklesbys were lucky they went to Roy instead of to someone who would really soak them. There were months when he didn't have anything to show them, no work to do. Some guys . . . and some women . . . would've made things up to pad the file."

It was a relief to find that Roy was as honest as I'd always thought him, after Jack's obvious admiration at Aunt Betty's creative lying. There was a separation, thank God, between lying on the job and relating to people in real life.

"What do you *know*?" I asked him, my fear finally showing in my voice.

"I know that the O'Shea girl is adopted, at least that's what the O'Sheas' neighbors in Philadelphia recall."

I remembered the slight change in Jess O'Shea's face when I'd asked him how the big-city hospital had been different from the tiny one in Bartley.

"You've been to Pennsylvania?"

"Their Philadelphia neighbors were seminary students like Jess, so naturally they've scattered. I've used other PIs in Florida, Kentucky, and Indiana. According to the people who'd talk to us, the O'Sheas arranged to adopt the baby girl of the sister of another seminary student. The O'Sheas had gotten a pretty discouraging work-up from a fertility specialist in Philadelphia. The sister had to give the baby up because she was in late-stage AIDS. Her family wouldn't take the baby because they believed the baby might be carrying the disease. It didn't matter that the baby had tested negative. In fact, the couple in Tennessee, the one I interviewed myself, are still convinced the little girl might have been 'carrying' AIDS, despite the testing the doctors did."

I shook my head. "How do you get people to tell you this?"

"I'm persuasive, in case you hadn't noticed." Jack ran his hand down my leg and leered at me. Then he sobered.

"So why are the O'Sheas still on your list?"

"One, Krista O'Shea is in the picture that Roy got. Two, what if this isn't the same girl they adopted?"

"What?"

"What if the tests were wrong? What if that child was born with AIDS, or died from some other cause? What if Lou O'Shea abducted Summer Dawn to take her place? What if the O'Sheas bought her?"

"That seems so far-fetched. They were up in Philadelphia for at least a few months after they adopted Krista. Summer Dawn was abducted in Conway, right?"

"Yes. But the O'Sheas have cousins living in the Conway area, cousins they visited when Jess finished the seminary. The dates coincide. So I can't rule them out. It's circumstantially possible. If they bought Summer Dawn from someone who abducted her, they would know that was illegal. They maybe pretended the baby was the one they'd adopted."

"What about Anna?" I asked sharply.

"Judy Kingery, Dill's first wife, was mentally ill."

I'd resumed studying the pictures. I turned to stare at Jack.

"Her auto accident was almost certainly suicide." His clear hazel eyes peered at me over his reading glasses.

"Oh, poor Dill." No wonder he'd taken his time dating Varena. He would be extra cautious after a hellish marriage like that, yoked to a woman with so many problems after his upbringing by a woman who was not exactly compos mentis.

"We can't be sure the wife didn't do something crazy. Maybe she killed their own baby and stole Summer Dawn as compensation. The Kingerys were living in Conway at the time the baby was taken. Maybe Judy Kingery snatched Summer Dawn and gave Dill some incredibly persuasive story."

"You're saying . . . it might be possible that Dill didn't know?"

Jack shrugged. "It's possible," he said but not with any great conviction.

I blew out a deep breath of tension. "OK, Eve Osborn."

"The Osborns moved here from a little town on the interstate about ten miles from Conway. He's worked at furniture stores since he got out of junior college. Meredith Osborn didn't make it through a whole year of college before she married him. Emory Ted Osborn . . ." Jack was peering through his glasses at a page of notes. "Emory sells furniture and appliances at Makepeace Furniture Center. Oh, I told you that when I told you Betty went to meet him there."

Makepeace Furniture Center was Bartley's best. It sold only upscale furniture and appliances, and it was located on the town square, having gradually crept through two or three buildings on one side.

"Emory have any criminal record?"

Jack shook his head. "None of these people do."

"Surely there's something that excludes Eve Osborn?"

"You know her?"

"Yes, I do. The Osborns own the little place my sister lives in. It's right in back of their house."

"I've driven by. I didn't realize your sister rented the cottage."

"Did you know that Meredith Osborn baby-sits both Anna and Krista from time to time? I met the mother and the little girl, Eve, when I was at Varena's a couple of days ago."

"What did you think?"

"There's a new baby, a girl. Mrs. Osborn is about as big as some twelve-year-olds, and she seems nice enough. Eve is a . . . well, a little girl, maybe a little shy. Real thin, like her mother. I haven't met Emory."

"He's small, too, thin and blond. He's got that really fair coloring, light blue eyes, invisible eyelashes. Looks like he still doesn't have to shave. Very reserved. Smiles a lot."

"So, where was Eve born?"

"That's why she can't be eliminated. Eve was a home birth," Jack said, both eyebrows raised as far as they could go. "Emory delivered her. He'd had some paramedic training. The baby evidently came too fast for them to get to the hospital."

"Meredith had the baby at her house?" Though I knew

historically that women had been having their babies at home far longer than they'd had them in hospitals, the idea jarred me.

"Yep." Jack's face expressed such distaste that I found myself hoping Jack was never trapped in a stalled elevator with a pregnant woman.

We stayed snuggled in the bed and each other's warmth a while more, talking ourselves in circles. I could not make this go away, and I could not stop Jack from investigating, even if I thought that right . . . which I didn't. I had tremendous pity for the anguished parents who had been wanting their child for so many years, and I had pity for my sister, whose life might be ruined in the three days before her wedding. There didn't seem to be anything I could do to affect the outcome of Jack's investigation.

It had been a long day.

I thought of the scene in the doctor's office, the devastation that had visited the two aging workhorses in their old office.

Wrapping my arms around my knees, I told Jack about Dr. LeMay and Mrs. Armstrong. He listened with close attention and asked me a lot more questions than I could answer.

"Do you think this could be connected with what you're investigating?" I asked.

"I don't see how." He took off his glasses, put them on the night table. "But it does seem like quite a coincidence that they're killed this week, just when I come on the scene, just when there's a new development in the Macklesby case. I've tried to be very discreet, but sooner or later in a town this size, everyone's gonna know why I'm here. You're providing me with cover right now, but it won't last if I ask the wrong questions."

I looked at Jack's watch then and slid out the bed. The room felt even colder after I'd been warmed by Jack. I wanted more than anything to lie beside him tonight, but I couldn't.

"I have to get back," I said, pulling on my clothes and trying to make them look as neat and straight as they had been earlier.

Jack got out of bed, too, but not as rapidly.

"I guess you have to," he said with an attempt at wistfulness.

"You know I have to go to their house tonight," I said, but not harshly. He'd pulled his slacks on by then. I was putting on my jacket when he began kissing me again. I tried to push him away when he made his first pass, but at his second, I put my arms around him.

"I know that you having gotten the implant, me not using a condom anymore, means you know I'm sleeping only with you," he told me.

It meant something else, too. "Ah . . . it means I'm not sleeping with anyone else, either," I reminded him.

After a moment of pregnant silence, he squeezed me so tightly I could not breathe, and he made an inarticulate noise. Suddenly I knew we were feeling exactly the same thing—just for a second, a flash, but it was a flash so bright it blinded me.

Then we had to bounce away from each other, frightened by the intimacy. Jack swung away to put on his shirt; I sat down to slide my feet into my shoes. I ran my fingers through my hair, took care of a button I'd skipped.

We were silent on the ride to my house, the bitter cold biting into our bones. When we pulled into the driveway I saw one light burning on the dimmest setting, in the living room. Jack leaned over to give me a quick kiss, and I was out of the car in a wink, running across the frosty lawn to the front door.

I locked the door behind me and went to the picture window. Looking out the small triangle unobscured by the Christmas tree, I saw Jack's car back out and start back to the motel. The sheets of his bed would smell like me.

Once in my room, where my mother had left a lamp on, I slowly undressed. It was too late to shower; it might wake my parents, if they weren't in their room lying awake to make sure I was home safe, like they'd done when I was a teenager. There was no counting the sleepless nights I'd given them.

Fleetingly, I thought about Teresa and Simon Macklesby. How many good nights' rest had they managed in the eight years since their daughter had vanished?

The murders of the doctor and his nurse, the strain of the wedding rehearsal, and the shock of all Jack had told me should have kept me awake. But being with Jack had drained the tension from me. Even if we hadn't had sex, I thought with some surprise, I would have felt better. I crawled in my bed, turned on my side, slid my hand under the pillow, and was immediately asleep.

The next day I had showered and dressed before I came out to have some coffee and breakfast. I'd done some sit-ups and leg lifts in my room so I wouldn't feel like a slug the rest of the day. My parents were both at the table, sections of newspaper propped up, when I got a mug from the cabinet.

"Good morning," my mother said with a smile.

My father grunted and nodded.

"How was your date last night?" Mother ventured when I was sitting with them.

"Fine," I said. My toast popped up, and I put it on a plate.

Dad peered over his glasses at me. "Got home late," he observed.

"Yes."

"How long you been dating this man? Your mother says you told her he was a private detective? Isn't that kind of dangerous?"

I answered the safest question. "I've been dating him for a few weeks."

"You think he might be serious?"

"Sometimes."

My father regarded me with some exasperation. "Now, what does that mean?"

"I think it means she doesn't want to answer any more questions, Gerald," Mother said. She rubbed the bridge of her nose with her thumb and forefinger, hiding a little smile.

"A father needs to know about men who are seeing his girl," my father said.

"This girl is almost thirty-two," I reminded him, trying to keep my voice gentle.

He shook his head. "I don't believe it. Why, that would make me *old*, gosh dog it!"

We all laughed as the little touchy moment passed.

Dad got up to shave, following his nearly invariable

morning routine. He stuck his head back in the door just as I bit into my toast. "Can you make any kind of living as a detective?" he asked, then hurried away before I could either laugh or throw my toast at him.

"The paper says," my mother began when I'd finished my coffee, "that Dave LeMay and Binnie Armstrong were killed right before you and Varena found them."

"I thought so," I said after a pause.

"You touched them?"

"Varena did. She's the nurse," I said, reminding my mother that I was not the only one present when awful things happened.

"That's true," my mother said slowly, as one who has received a revelation of which she's half proud, half dismayed. "She has to deal with things like that all the time."

"That bad or worse." Once upon a time, Varena had given me a graphic description of a motorcycle rider who'd stretched out his arm at the wrong moment and come into the hospital without it. A passerby had had the presence of mind to wrap it in the blanket his dog sat on when it rode in the car and bring it into the hospital. I had seen bad things . . . maybe just as bad . . . but I didn't think I could have dealt calmly with that. Varena had been excited—not by the crisis but by her team's effective response.

Evidently she didn't talk about some aspects of being a nurse, at least to our mother.

"I never quite pictured her job that way." Mother looked thoughtful, as if she were seeing her younger daughter in a different light.

I read the comics for a minute or two, Ann Landers, the horoscopes, the scrambled words, the "find the errors" drawing. I never had time to do this at home. Thank God.

"What's on the agenda today?" I asked, without feeling one bit excited. The pleasure of Jack's presence in town had faded, to be replaced by the gnawing anxiety of his suspicions.

"Oh, there's the shower at Grace's in the afternoon, but this morning we have to go to Corbett's to pick up a few things they called us about."

Corbett's was the town's premier gift shop. Every bride with any claim to class went to Corbett's to register her china and silver patterns, and also to indicate a range of acceptable colors that would look good in the bride's future kitchen and bath. Corbett's also carried small appliances, pricey kitchenware, and sheets and table linens. Many brides left an all-encompassing list at Corbett's. Varena and I had always called it the "I want it" list.

Two hours later—two dragging, boring hours later—we were in Varena's car, parallel parking on Bartley's town square. The old post office crumbled on one side, while the courthouse, in the center on a manicured lawn, was festooned with Christmas decorations. Unlike Shakespeare, Bartley was holding on to its manger scene, though I had never found plastic figures in a wooden shed exactly spiritual. Carols blared endlessly from the speakers located around the square, and all the merchants had lined their store windows with twinkling colored lights and artificial snow.

If there was a true religious emotion to be felt about Christmas, I had been too numbed by all this claptrap to feel it for the past three years.

I was glad to see Varena click the "lock" button on her key-ring control, and the car gave its little *honk!* to show it had received her command. Naturally we all looked at the car as it made the sound, a senseless but natural reaction, and I almost didn't see the running man until too late.

He was coming for us out of nowhere, his hand already outstretched to grab my mother's purse, which she was clutching loosely under her right arm.

With a positive rush of pleasure, I planted my left foot, came up with my right knee, and flicked my foot out to catch him in the jaw. In real life (as opposed to movies) high kicks are risky and energy draining: The knee and the groin are much more reliable targets. But this was my chance to land a high kick, and I took it. Thanks to hours and hours of practice, my instep smacked his jaw correctly, and he staggered. I got him again on the way down, though it was not as effective an impact. It hastened his fall rather than damaging him further.

He managed to land on his knees, and I seized his right arm and twisted it sharply behind him. He screamed and hit the pavement, and I kept his arm behind and up at an angle I knew to be extremely painful. I was on his right, out of reach of his left hand if he could manage to lever himself up to grab for my ankle.

"I'll break your arm if you move," I told him sincerely.

He believed me. He lay on the sidewalk, panting for breath—sobbing for breath, really.

I glanced up to see my mother and sister staring not at their assailant but at me, with stunned amazement making their faces foolish.

"Call the police," I prompted them.

Varena kind of jumped and ran into Corbett's. She was doing a lot of police calling these days. The Bard sisters were on a roll.

The man I'd downed was short, stocky, black. He had

on a ragged coat, and he smelled. I figured this was probably the same man who'd taken Diane Dykeman's purse a
couple of days ago.

"Let me up, bitch," he said now, having gathered enough
breath to speak.

"Be polite," I said, my voice harsh. I gave his arm a yank
upward, and he screamed.

"Oh, Lily," my mother gasped. "Oh, honey. Do you
have to . . . ?" Her voice trailed off as I looked up to meet her
eyes.

"Yes," I said. "I have to."

A siren went off right behind me. The patrol officer
must have been two blocks away when he got the call from
the dispatcher, so he put on his siren. It nearly made me lose
my grip. The car had "Bartley Police Department" printed
in an arc over the Bartley town symbol, some complicated
mishmash involving cotton and tractors. Under the symbol,
the word "Chief" was centered in large letters.

"What we got here?" called the man in the uniform as he
bounded up on the sidewalk. He had brown hair and a neat
mustache. He was lean except for a curious potbelly, like a
five-month pregnancy. He looked at the man on the sidewalk, at my grip on his arm.

"Hey, Lily," he said, after assessing all this. "What you
got here?"

"Chandler?" I said, peering up at his face. "Chandler
McAdoo?"

"In the flesh," he drawled. "You caught you a purse
snatcher?"

"So it seems."

"Hi, Miz Bard," Chandler said, nodding at my mother,
who nodded back automatically. I looked up at her shocked

face, thinking as I did so that nothing could make her feel better for a little bit. Being the victim of a random crime was a shocking experience.

Chandler McAdoo had been my lab partner in high school, one memorable semester. We had done the frog thing together. I had been holding the knife—or the scalpel? I couldn't remember—and I had been on the verge of going silly-girl squeamish, when Chandler had looked me straight in the eye and told me I was a weak and useless critter if I couldn't cut one little hole in a dead frog.

He was right, I had figured, and I had cut.

That wasn't the only thing Chandler McAdoo had dared me to do, but it was the only dare I'd taken.

Chandler bent over now with his handcuffs, and with a practiced move, he had my prisoner cuffed before the man knew what was happening. I rose, with a courteous assist from Chief Chandler, and while I was telling him what had happened, he hauled the cuffed man to his feet and propelled the prisoner toward the squad car.

He listened, made a call on his radio.

I stared at every move he made, unable to square this man, this police chief with his severe haircut and cool eyes, with the boy who'd gotten drunk with me on Rebel Yell.

"Where you think he came from?" Chandler asked, as if it weren't too important. My mother had been coaxed inside the store by Varena and the sales clerks.

"Must have been there," I decided, pointing at the alley running between Corbett's and the furniture store. "That's the only place he could've been hiding unseen." It was a narrow alley, and if he'd been just a few feet inside it, he would have been invisible. "Where was Diane Dykeman when her purse was snatched?"

Chandler cocked an eye at me. "She was over by Dill's pharmacy, two blocks away," he said. "The snatcher dodged back in the alley, and we couldn't track him. I don't see how we could have missed this guy, but I guess he could have hidden until we'd checked the alley behind the store. There are more little niches and hidey-holes in this downtown area than you can shake a stick at."

I nodded. Since the downtown area of Bartley was more than a hundred and fifty years old, during which time the Square businesses had flourished and gone broke in cycles, I could well believe it.

"You stay put," Chandler said and strode down the alley. I sighed and stayed put. I glanced at my watch once or twice. He was gone for seven minutes.

"I think he's been sleeping back there," Chandler said when he reemerged onto the sidewalk. Suddenly my high school buddy was galvanized, and there wasn't any languid small-town-cop air about him anymore. "I didn't find Diane's purse, but there're some refrigerator cartons and a nest of rags."

Chandler had that saving-the-punchline air. He bent into his car and used the radio again.

"I just called Brainerd, who answered the call on the murder cases," he told me after he straightened. "Come look."

I followed Chandler down the alley. We arrived at the T junction, where this little alley joined the larger one running behind the buildings on the west of the square. There was a refrigerator carton tucked into a niche behind some bushes that had made their precarious lives in the cracks in the rough pavement. Chandler pointed, and I followed his finger to see a length of rusty pipe close to but not visible from the carton, as I figured it. The pipe had been placed on a broken drain that had formerly run from the top of the flat-roofed furniture store to the gutter, and the placement rendered it all but invisible if it had not been stained at one end. The pipe, more than two feet long and about two inches in diameter, was darker at one end than the other.

"Bloodstains?" Chandler said. "Dave LeMay, I'm thinking."

I stared at the pipe again and understood.

The same man who might have beaten to death the doctor and his nurse had come that close to my *mother*. For a savage second, I wished I had kicked him harder and longer. I could have broken his arm, or his skull so easily while I had him down on the sidewalk. I stared out of the alley. I could just glimpse the man's profile as he sat in Chandler's car. That face was vacant. Nobody home.

"You go on in the store, Lily," Chandler said, maybe reading my face too easily. "Your mama might need you right now, Varena too. We'll talk later."

I spun on my heel and strode down the alley to the street, to enter the glass-paned front door of Corbett's. A bell attached to the door tinkled, and the little crowd around my mother shifted to absorb me.

There was a couch positioned opposite the Bride's Area, where all the local brides' and grooms' selections of china and silverware were displayed. Mother was sitting on that sofa, Varena beside her explaining what had happened.

Another police car pulled to the curb outside, spurring more activity. Amid all the bustle, the telephoning, and the concern on the faces of the women around her, my mother gradually recovered her color and composure. When she knew Mom was okay, Varena took me aside and gripped my arm.

"Way to go, Sis," she said.

I shrugged.

"You did good."

I almost shrugged again and looked away. But instead I ventured a smile.

And Varena smiled back.

"Hey, I hate to interrupt this sister-sister talk," Chandler said, sticking his head in the shop door, "but I gotta take statements from you three."

So we all went down to the little Bartley police station, one block away, to make our statements. What had happened had been so quick and simple, really just a matter of a few seconds, that it didn't take long. As we left, Chandler reminded us to stop by the station the next day to sign our statements.

Chandler motioned me to remain. I obediently lagged behind. I looked curiously at him. He didn't, wouldn't, meet my eyes.

"They ever catch 'em, Lily?"

The back of my neck prickled and tightened. "No," I said.

"Damn." And back into his tiny office he strode, all the equipment he wore on his belt making every step a statement of certainty. I took a deep breath and hurried to catch up with Mom and Varena.

We still had to go back to Corbett's Gift Shop. The women in my family weren't going to let a little thing like an attempted theft deter them from their appointed rounds. So we slid back into our little wedding groove. Varena got the basket full of presents she'd come to pick up, Mother accepted compliments on Varena's impending marriage, I was patted on the back (though somewhat gingerly) for stopping the purse snatcher, and when my adrenaline jolt finally expired . . . I was back to being bored.

We drove home to open and record the presents. While Mother and Varena told Daddy about our unexpectedly exciting shopping expedition, I wandered into the living room and stared out the front window. I switched on the Christmas tree lights, found that they blinked, shut them off.

I wondered what Jack was doing.

I found myself thinking about the homeless man I'd kicked. I thought of the redness of his eyes, the stubble on his face, his dishevelment, his smell. Would Dr. LeMay have remained seated behind his desk if such a man had come into his office? I didn't think so.

And Dr. LeMay must have died first. If he'd heard Binnie Armstrong speaking to an unknown man, Binnie being attacked, he would *never* have been caught sitting. He would have been up and around the desk, struggling, despite his age. He had been a proud man, a man's man.

If that sad specimen had made his way into the doctor's office when it was officially closed, Dr. LeMay would have shown him the door, or told him to make an appointment, or called the police, or referred him to the emergency room doctor who drove out from Pine Bluff every day. Dave LeMay would have dealt with the homeless man any number of ways.

But he wouldn't have stayed behind his desk.

The intruder would have had the pipe in his hands. He hadn't come upon a rusty pipe in the doctor's office. And if the intruder had entered with the pipe, he had *intended* to kill Dr. LeMay and Mrs. Armstrong.

I shook my head as I stared out the living room window. I was not a law enforcement officer or any kind of detective, but several things about the homeless-man-as-murderer scenario just didn't make sense. And the more I thought about it, the fishier it seemed: If the homeless man had killed Dr. LeMay and Mrs. Armstrong, why hadn't he robbed the place? Could the horror of what he'd done have driven him out before he accomplished his purpose?

If he was innocent, how had the murder weapon—what Chandler McAdoo seemed to think was the murder weapon—come to be in the alley? If this man was clever enough to hide Diane Dykeman's purse, which he almost certainly had stolen, why hadn't he been clever enough to get rid of the evidence of a much more serious crime?

I'll tell you what I'd do, I thought. If I wanted to commit a murder and pin it on a throwaway person, I'd put the murder weapon right by a homeless man, moreover a black homeless man . . . someone with no local ties, no likely alibi, and already reported to be a purse snatcher.

That's what I'd do.

The back door to the doctor's office had been locked, I recalled. So the murderer had come in the front, as Varena and I had. He had walked past the doorway of the room in which Mrs. Armstrong was working, and she had *not been alarmed.* Binnie Armstrong had been lying in the doorway, so she had calmly continued whatever she had been doing in the little lab.

So. The murderer—carrying the pipe—walks into the office, which is officially closed. The murderer passes Binnie

Armstrong, who stays right where she is. Then the murderer had gone into Dr. LeMay's office, looked at the old man on the other side of the piled desk, spoken to him. Though the killer had had a length of pipe in one hand, *still* the doctor hadn't been alarmed.

I felt goosebumps shiver down my arms.

Without warning—since Dr. LeMay was still in his chair, which was still pushed right up to the desk—the murderer had lifted the pipe and hit Dr. LeMay over the head, kept hitting him, until he was just tissue. Then the killer had stepped out into the hall, and while Binnie was hurrying from the lab to investigate the awful sounds she'd heard, he hit her, too . . . until she was on the verge of death.

Then he'd stepped out the front door and gotten into his vehicle . . . but surely he must have been covered in blood?

I frowned. Here was a snag. Even the most angelic of white men could not step out in front of the doctor's office in the daytime with blood-soaked clothing, carrying a bloody pipe.

"Lily?" My mother's voice. "Lily?"

"Yes?"

"I thought we'd have an early lunch, since the shower is this afternoon."

"OK." I tried to control the lurch of my stomach at the thought of food.

"It's on the table. I've called you twice."

"Oh. Sorry." As I reluctantly dipped my spoon into my mother's homemade beef soup, I tried to get back on my train of thought, but it had rolled out of the station.

Here we all were, sitting around the kitchen table, just as we had for so many years.

Suddenly, this scene seemed overwhelmingly bleak. *Here we still were,* the four of us.

"Excuse me, I have to walk," I said, pushing away from the table. The three of them looked up at me, a familiar dismay dragging at their mouths. But the compulsion had gotten so strong that I could no longer play my part.

I threw on my coat, pulled on gloves as I left the house.

The first block was bliss. Even in the freezing cold, even in the face of the sharp wind, I was by myself. At least the sun was shining in its watery winter way, and the clear colors of the pines and holly bushes against the pale blue sky made my eyes blink with pleasure. The branches of the hardwood trees looked like a bleak version of lace. Our neighbor's big brown dog barked and trailed my progress for the length of his yard, but he stopped at that and gave me no more trouble. I remembered I had to nod when cars went past, but in Bartley that was not so frequent, even at lunchtime.

I turned a corner to put the wind behind me, and in time I passed the Presbyterian church and the manse, where the O'Sheas lived. I wondered if the toddler, Luke, was letting Lou sleep. But I couldn't think about the O'Sheas without thinking of the picture that Roy Costimiglia had received in the mail.

Whoever sent that picture obviously knew which girl was the abducted Summer Dawn Macklesby. That particular picture, attached to that particular article, sent to the Macklesbys' PI, was intended to lead Roy Costimiglia to one conclusion. Why hadn't the anonymous sender gone one step farther and circled the child's face? Why the ambiguity?

That was a real puzzle.

Of course . . . if you could figure out who'd sent it . . . you could find out why. Maybe.

Great piece of detection, Lily, I told myself scornfully, and walked even faster. A brown mailing envelope that could be bought at any Wal-Mart, a picture from a yearbook that hundreds of students had purchased . . . well, one copy would be missing that page now. Page 23, I remembered, from looking so hard at the one in Jack's briefcase.

Of course, the whole thing was really Jack's problem. Furthermore, it was a problem Jack was being paid to solve.

But I needed to know the answer before Varena married Dill Kingery. And the fact was evident that, though Jack was a trained and dogged detective, I was the one on the inside track, here in Bartley.

So I tried to imagine some way I could help Jack, some information I could discover for him.

I couldn't think of a damn thing I could do.

But maybe something would come to me.

The harder and longer I walked, the better I felt. I was breathing easier: The claustrophobia induced by family closeness was loosening its knot.

I glanced at my watch and stopped dead in my tracks.

It was time for Varena's shower.

Luckily, I had been meandering around in my parents' neighborhood, so I was only four blocks away from their house. I set out quickly, arriving at the front door within minutes. They'd left it unlocked, which was a relief. I dashed to my bedroom, skinned out of my jeans and sweater, and pulled on my black pants–blue blouse–black jacket combination. I checked the shower location and dashed out the door.

I was only ten minutes late.

This was a kitchen shower at the home of Mother's best friend, Grace Parks. Grace lived on a street of large homes, and hers was one of the largest. She had daily help, I remembered, and I cast a professional eye over the house as I entered.

You wouldn't catch Grace looking relieved to see me, but the lines bracketing her generous mouth did relax when I came in. She gave me a ritual hug and a pat on the shoulder that was just a little too forceful, as she told me my mother and sister were in the living room waiting for me. I'd always liked Grace, who would be blond until the day she died. Grace seemed indestructible. Her brown eyes were always made up, her curvy figure had never sagged (at least on the surface), and she wore magnificent jewelry quite routinely.

She slid me into a chair she'd saved right by my mother and answered a question from one of the assembled guests even as she was putting the pencil and notepad in my hands. I stared at it blankly for a moment until I realized I'd been assigned the task of recording the gifts and givers.

I gave Mom a cautious smile, and she cautiously smiled back. Varena gave me a compound look, irritation and relief mixed in equal parts. "Sorry," I said quietly.

"You made it," my mother said, her voice calm and matter-of-fact.

I nodded at the circle of women in Grace's huge living room, recognizing most of them from the shower two days ago. These people would be just as relieved as Varena to have the wedding over with. More people seemed to have been invited to this shower; maybe since Grace had such a large home, she'd told Varena to expand the basic guest list.

Because I'd been thinking of their daughters, I particularly noticed Meredith Osborn and Lou O'Shea. Mrs. Kingery was sitting on the other side of Varena, which was a relief. It seemed unfair to me that Dill should have such a nerve-wracking mother after his wife had been unstable enough to kill herself. I could see why he'd be attracted to Varena, who had always seemed to be one of the most stable and balanced people I'd ever known.

It was the first time I'd realized that. It's strange how you can know someone all your life and still not spell out her strong and weak points to yourself.

This shower had a kitchen theme. All the guests had been asked to include their favorite recipe with their gift. As we began the grand opening, I got busy. My handwriting is not elegant, but it is clear, and I tried to do a thorough job. Some boxes were stuffed with little things rather than a single gift, like a set of dish towels. Diane Dykeman (she of the snatched purse) had given Varena a set of measuring spoons and measuring cups, a little scale, and a chart of weight equivalencies, and I had to use my most microscopic writing to enter everything.

This was really an excellent job to have, I decided, because I didn't have to talk to anyone. The story about me kicking the purse snatcher wasn't town currency yet, and Mother and Varena were avoiding the subject. But I was pretty sure it would begin to make the rounds when time came for refreshments.

When that moment arrived—when all the gifts had been opened and Grace Parks had vanished for a significant time—she reappeared at my elbow and asked me to pour the punch.

It occurred to me that Grace understood me pretty well. I gave her an assessing look as I took my place at one end of her massive oval dining table, polished to a gleaming shine, bisected by a Christmas runner and covered with the usual shower food: nuts, cake, finger sandwiches, mints, snack mix.

"You're like me," Grace said. She gave me a direct look. "You like to be busy more than you like to sit and listen."

It had never crossed my mind that I was in any way like the elegant Grace Parks. I nodded and began to fill my ladle for the first one around the table—Varena, of course, the honoree.

I had to do no more than say "Punch?" after that and smile and nod.

After a long time, it was over, and once again we loaded gifts into the car, thanked Grace profusely, and drove home to unload.

After I'd changed back to jeans and the sweater, Varena asked me if I'd go to her cottage with her to help pack. She'd been moving her things slowly into Dill's house over the past month, beginning with the things she needed least.

Of course I agreed, relieved both at the prospect of being busy and of being helpful. We had a quick sandwich and went over to the cottage, with a few stops along the way. Dill, Varena told me, was spending some quality time with Anna, who'd been showing signs of being overwhelmed by all the wedding excitement.

"I've reached the point where all I can do here at my place is sleep," she told me, after she'd put her sweats on. "But I kept the lease up until the end of December, because I really didn't want to move back in with the folks." I nodded. I could see that once she did that, she and Dill would have lost whatever privacy they had. Or did Varena just want to ensure she had a break from our parents?

"What do you have left to pack?"

Varena began to open closets, showing me what she hadn't managed to empty out before now.

We'd stopped behind some stores to collect boxes. Downtown had been empty, now that most of the businesses were closed. It was fully dark at six o'clock this time of year, and the night was very cold. The cottage seemed warm and homey in contrast to the blackness outside.

I was assigned to pack the tiny closet by the front door, which contained things like extra lightbulbs, extension cords, batteries, and the vacuum cleaner. As I began to pack them in a sturdy box, Varena started wrapping some pots and pans with newspaper. We worked in comfortable silence for a little while.

Varena had just asked me if I wanted some instant hot chocolate when we heard the sound of someone walking outside the cottage.

The scare we'd had that morning must have made us jumpy. Both of us raised our heads like deer hearing the sound of the hunter's boots. Peripherally, I saw Varena turn to me, but I shook my head slightly to make her keep silent.

Then someone kicked the front door.

Varena shrieked.

"Who is it?" I called, standing to one side of the door.

"Jack," he yelled. "Let me in!"

I caught my breath in a rattling gasp, frightened and furious at being so. I yanked the door open, ready to let him know how much I appreciated being jolted like that. The words died in my throat when I opened the door. Jack was carrying Meredith Osborn. She was covered in blood.

Behind me I heard Varena pick up the phone, punch in 911. She spoke tersely to whoever answered.

Jack was haggard with shock. Some of Meredith Osborn's blood was smeared on him. He was breathing raggedly. Though she was a small woman, he'd been carrying her as a dead weight.

Varena picked up a sheet she'd just folded and flung it over the couch in one movement, and Jack gladly laid the little woman down. When he'd deposited his burden he stood for a moment with his arms still curved. Then with a groan he straightened them, his shoulders moving unconsciously in an effort to relax strained muscles.

Varena was already on her knees beside the couch, her hands on her landlady's wrist. She was shaking her head.

"She's got a pulse, but it's . . ." Varena shook her head again. "She's been lying outside." The dying woman's face was ice-white, and the cold was rolling off the tiny body, eddying through the warm room.

We heard the sound of the ambulance in the distance.

Meredith Osborn opened her eyes. They fixed on mine.

Someone had struck her across her face, and her lips were cracked, had bled. Underneath the blood, they were blue, to match the tinge of her fingernails.

Her mouth opened. "The children," she whispered.

"Don't worry," Varena said instantly. "They're fine."

Meredith Osborn turned her gaze from my face to Varena's. Her mouth moved again. She tried as hard as she could to tell Varena something.

Instead, she died.

FIVE

I held on to Jack. He held on to me. We'd seen people die—bad people, violent people, people who had the misfortune to be in the wrong place at the wrong time. This young woman, newly a mother, beaten and left in the freezing air, was something else again.

It was Varena who ran over to the Osborn house to see if the children were there, Varena who discovered that the house was empty and silent. And, twenty minutes later, it was Varena who saw the car with Emory Osborn, Eve, and the baby Jane pull into the driveway, to be met with the news that would change their lives forever.

Lanky Detective Brainerd was on duty again, or still on duty, and he eyed me dubiously, even after we explained what had happened.

"What were you doing here?" he asked Jack directly. "I don't believe you're from here, sir."

"No, sir, I'm not. I'm here to visit Lily, and I'm staying

at the Delta Motel." Jack let go of me and stepped closer to Brainerd.

I kept my gaze on the floor. I didn't know if Jack was making a mistake or not, keeping his business in Bartley a secret.

"How'd you know Miss Bard was here?"

"Her car is here," Jack said.

It was true, we'd come in my car. Mother had taken Varena to the wedding shower, so I'd given her a ride from their place over to the cottage.

After her burst of energy, Varena was slumped in an armchair, staring into space.

"So you stopped here to see Miss Bard . . . ?"

"And when I got out of the car, I thought I heard a noise from behind the big house," Jack said calmly. "So I thought I'd check it out before I alarmed Lily and Varena."

"You found Mrs. Osborn."

"Yes. She was lying between the back of the house and their garage."

"Did she speak to you?"

"No."

"She said nothing?"

"No. She didn't seem to know I'd picked her up."

"But she spoke when she was lying on the couch?"

"Yes," I said.

Jack and Detective Brainerd turned simultaneously.

"And what did she say?" the policeman asked.

"She said, 'The children.' "

"And that's all?"

"That's all."

Brainerd looked thoughtful, as well he might.

What had Meredith Osborn meant? Had the last

thoughts of the dying woman simply been dwelling on the children she was leaving behind? Or did those words mean more? Were her two children in danger? Or was she thinking of the three girls in the picture?

Whoever had sent the picture to Jack's friend Roy had started a deadly train of events.

After the ambulance removed Meredith's body, I stared out the side window of Varena's cottage, watching the police search the backyard where she had lain bleeding and freezing.

I was full of anger.

The death of Meredith Osborn had not even had the mercy of being fast. Dave LeMay and Binnie Armstrong had had only moments to fear death—and those were dreadful moments, I fully appreciated that, believe me. But lying in your own backyard, unable to summon help, feeling your own end creeping through you . . . I closed my eyes, felt myself shudder. I knew something about hours of fear, about being certain your death was imminent and unavoidable. I had been spared, finally. Meredith Osborn had not.

Jack put an arm around my shoulder.

"I want to go away," I whispered.

I couldn't, and we both knew it.

"Excuse me," I said at a more conversational volume, hearing my voice's coldness. "I'm being silly."

Jack sighed. "I wish I could go away, too."

"What killed her?"

"Not a gun. Knife wounds, I think."

I shivered. I hated knives.

"Did we bring this here with us, Jack?" I whispered.

"No," he said. "This was here before we came. But it won't be here when I leave." When Jack got his teeth into something, he didn't let go, even when he was biting the wrong part.

"Tomorrow," I told him, quietly. "Tomorrow we'll talk."

"Yes."

I was taking Varena home to spend the night. She couldn't sleep in this cottage. She was ready, standing staring out the side window at the lit backyard, the figures moving around it. So I tried to walk out the door. But after I'd stepped away from Jack I reached back to grip his wrist. I couldn't seem to let go. I looked down at my feet, struggling with myself.

"Lily?" Under the questioning tone, his voice was hoarse.

I bit my lip, hard.

"I'm gone," I said, letting go of him. "I'll see you in the morning, at eight. At the motel." I glanced at his face.

He nodded.

"Lock her cottage when the police let you go, OK?"

Varena didn't seem to hear us. She stood like a statue at that window, her overnight bag on the floor beside her.

"Sure," he said, still looking intently at me.

"Then I'll see you tomorrow," I said and turned my back on him and walked out, beckoning to my sister to follow.

I have done so many hard things, but that was one of the hardest.

It was only nine by the time we got to my parents' house, but it felt like midnight. I didn't want to see anyone or talk to anyone, and yet somehow my parents had to be told, had to be talked to. Luckily for me, Varena had regained her balance by the time she saw my mother, and though she cried a little, she managed to relate the horrible death of Meredith Osborn.

"Should I just cancel the wedding?" she asked tearfully.

I knew my mother would talk her out of it. I really couldn't bear to be with people right now. I went to my room and shut the door firmly. My father came to stand outside in the hall; I knew his footsteps.

"Are you okay, pumpkin?" he called.

"Yes."

"Do you want to be alone?"

I clenched my fists until even my short fingernails bit into my palms. "Yes, please."

"OK." Off he went, God bless him.

I lay on the hard bed, hands clasped across my stomach, and thought.

I could not imagine how I could find out any more information about the three girls who might be Summer Dawn. But I was convinced that Meredith Osborn's death had come about because she knew which girl was not who she seemed to be. I tried to picture Lou O'Shea or the Reverend O'Shea attacking Meredith in the freezing cold of her backyard, but I just could not. Still less could I imagine mild Dill Kingery stabbing Meredith into silence. Dill's mother was certainly off-base, but I'd never seen any tendency to violence. Mrs. Kingery just seemed daffy.

I thought of Meredith Osborn taking care of Krista O'Shea and Anna Kingery. What could she have seen—or heard—that would lead her to think she knew that one of the girls had been born with a different identity?

I'd never had a baby, so I didn't know what happened bureaucratically when you gave birth. Some hospitals, I knew, took little footprints—I'd seen them framed on the walls of the Althaus family when I cleaned for them. And of course there was the birth certificate. And pictures. A lot of hospitals took pictures, for the parents. To me, all babies pretty much looked the same, red and scrunch-faced, or brown and scrunch-faced. That some had hair and some didn't was the only obvious distinction I could see.

I had learned, also from the much-birthed Carol Althaus, that the fingerprints police or volunteers sometimes took at mall booths were not helpful because often they were of poor quality. I didn't know if that was true, but it sounded reasonable. I was willing to bet the same reasons would render any existing baby footprints of Summer Dawn unusable.

So fingerprints and footprints were a no go. DNA testing could prove Summer Dawn's identity, I was sure, but of course you had to know whom to test. I couldn't see Jack demanding that the three girls undergo DNA testing. Well, I could see him demanding it, but I could also see all three sets of parents turning him down cold.

I stared at the ceiling until I realized my mind was going through the same cycle of thought, over and over, and it was no more productive than it had been the first time I'd gone through it.

I remembered, as I was undressing and pulling on a nightgown, that when Jack had first come to my bed, the next morning I'd made myself a promise: never to ask Jack for anything.

I was having a hard time keeping that promise.

As I lay once again on the bed I'd slept in as a virgin, I had to remind myself over and over that there was a corollary to that promise: not to offer what was not asked for.

I heard my sister next door in her old room, going

through the same motions I'd gone through. I was sure she was hurting, sure she was suffering doubly since this blood and gore was happening at the time that was supposed to be the happiest in her life.

I felt helpless.

It was the most galling feeling in the world.

I was up and out of the house the next morning before my parents were stirring. I couldn't wait for eight o'clock. I rose, took a hasty shower, and yanked on ordinary clothes, not much caring what they were as long as they were warm.

I started my car with a little difficulty and drove through the frosty streets. There were a few more cars at the motel, so my knock at Jack's door was quiet.

He opened it after just a second, and I stepped inside. Jack closed the door quickly behind me, shirtless and shivering in the gust of cold air that entered with me.

What I had been going to do, planning to do, was sit in one of the two uncomfortable vinyl-covered chairs while Jack sat in the other and discuss his plans and how I could help.

What happened was, the minute the door was closed we were on each other like hungry wolves. When I touched him, my hands were pleased with everything they encountered. When I kissed him, I wanted him instantly. I was shaking so hard with wanting him that I couldn't get my clothes off, and he pulled my sweatshirt over my head and yanked down my jeans and underwear, helping me step out of them, pulling me to the bed into his nest of residual warmth.

Afterward, we lay with our arms around each other. I didn't care that my left arm was going to sleep, he didn't seem to mind that there wasn't an altogether comfortable place for his right leg.

He whispered my name in my ear. I smoothed his hair, tangled and loose, back from his face. I ran my fingers over the stubble on his chin. There were words in my mouth that I would not say. I clamped my teeth over them and continued to touch him. That stupid, fragile, ludicrous swelling in my chest had to remain contained.

His hands were occupied, too, and after a few minutes we made love again, not as frantically. There was nothing I wanted so much as to stay in that sorry motel bed, as long as Jack was in it.

I was dressing (again) after another quick shower. "What are you going to do next?" I asked, hearing the reluctance in my voice.

"Find out which of the little girls had seen Dr. LeMay recently."

"I figured that had something to do with it. After all, the homeless man was in jail when Meredith Osborn was killed."

"She wasn't beaten like the doctor and his nurse." Jack had been brushing his hair back into its ponytail. Now he gave me a curious look. He was wearing a long-sleeved polo shirt striped rust and brown, and the scar that ran down his cheek to his jaw seemed whiter in contrast. He ran a belt through the loops on his khakis. "Might have been a different killer."

"Umhum," I said skeptically. "All of a sudden, Bartley is full of brutal murders. And you're trying to find a missing child. This is just coincidence."

He gave me the look that I'd learned meant he was up to

something: It was a sideways look, a quick flash of the eyes, to gauge my mood.

"The homeless man's name is Christopher Darby Sims."

"OK, I'll bite. How'd you know that?"

"I have a connection here at the police department."

I wondered uneasily if this was one of those good ole boy things, or if Jack meant he'd bribed a cop. Or perhaps both.

"So, can this connection look through the doctor's records?"

"I can't ask that much. I'm feeling my way. Are you still squeamish about frogs?" Jack asked, a little smile turning up the corners of his mouth.

"Chandler McAdoo."

Jack lifted a corner of the curtain, peered out at the bleak day and the depressing motel court. "I stopped by the police station yesterday. Once I mentioned your name and hinted pretty strongly that we were tight, Chandler began to talk to me. He's given me some fascinating stories about your teen years." He tried not to grin too broadly.

As long as Chandler hadn't told him about the later years. "I can't even remember what I was like then," I said. And I was speaking the literal truth. "I can remember some of the things we got up to," I said, smiling a little, tentatively. "But I can't for the life of me recall what I felt. Too much water under the bridge, I guess." It was like I could see a silent movie of my life without hearing sound or feeling emotion. I shrugged. What was gone, was gone.

"I'm memorizing some stories," Jack warned me. "And when you least expect it . . ."

I tightened my shoelaces, still smiling, and kissed Jack good-bye. "Call me when you know something or want me to do something," I told him. I felt the smile slide right off my mouth. "I want this over."

Jack nodded. "I do, too," he said, his voice even. "And then I never want to see Teresa and Simon Macklesby again."

I looked up at him, reading his face. I touched his cheek with my fingers. "You can do this," I said.

"Yeah, I should be able to," he told me, his voice bleak and empty.

"What's your program for the morning?" I asked.

"I'm helping Dill put a floor in his attic."

"What?"

"I just happened to be in the pharmacy yesterday afternoon and we were talking, and he told me that was what he was going to be doing this morning, no matter how cold it was. He wanted to get the job finished before the wedding. So I said I didn't have anything to do since you were wrapped up in wedding plans, and I'd be glad to lend him a hand."

"And ask him a few questions while you're at it?"

"Possibly." Jack smiled at me, that charming smile that coaxed so much information out of citizens.

I drove home, trying to think my way through a maze.

My family was up, Varena shaky but much better. They'd had a conference while I was gone and made up their minds to go through with the wedding no matter what. I was glad I'd missed that one, glad the decision had been made without me. If Varena had postponed her wedding, it would have made the time frame easier, but I had a concern I hadn't shared with Jack.

I was afraid—if the murderer of Dr. LeMay, Mrs. Armstrong, and Meredith Osborn was the same person—that this criminal was getting frantic. And a person frantically trying to conceal a crime was likely to kill the strongest link between him and the crime.

In this case, that would be Summer Dawn Macklesby.

On one level, it didn't seem likely that whoever'd gone to such extreme lengths to conceal the original crime—the abduction—would even consider killing the girl. But on another level, it seemed obvious, even likely.

I knew nothing that could help solve this crime. What did I know how to do? I knew how to clean and how to fight.

I also knew where people were most likely to hide things. Cleaning had certainly taught me that. Objects could be mislaid anywhere (though I had a mental list of places I checked first, when employers asked me to keep my eyes open for some missing item) but hidden . . . that was a different matter.

So? I asked myself sarcastically. How was that going to help?

"Could you, sweetheart?" my mother was saying.

"What?" I asked, my voice sharp and quick. She'd startled me.

"I'm sorry," my mother said, her voice making it clear I should be saying that to her. "I asked if you would mind going over to Varena's place and finishing her packing?"

I wasn't sure why I was being asked to do this. Was Varena too scared to be there by herself? And it wasn't supposed to bother me? But maybe I'd been woolgathering while they'd spelled it out.

Varena certainly looked as if she needed sleep and a holiday. And this, right before the happiest time of her life.

"Of course," I said. "What about the wedding dress?"

"Oh, my heavens!" Mother exclaimed. "We've got to

114

get that out right away!" Mother's pale face flushed. Somehow, the wedding dress was at risk in that apartment. Galvanized by this sudden urgency, Mother shooed me into my car and bundled herself up in record time.

She followed me over to Varena's and took the dress home personally, carrying it from the cottage to the car as though it were the crown and scepter of royalty.

I was left alone in Varena's place, an oddly unsettling feeling. It was like surreptitiously going through her drawers. I shrugged. I was here to do a job. That thought was very normal, very steadying, after all we'd seen lately.

I counted boxes, moved the ones already full out to my car trunk after labeling them with Varena's black marker. "Martha Stewart, that's me," I muttered and folded out the flaps on another box, placing it by the nearest closet. This was a little double closet with sliding doors in Varena's tiny hall. It held only a few linens and towels. I guessed Varena had already moved the others.

Just as I'd picked up the first handful, trying to restrain myself from shaking the sheets out and refolding them, there was a knock on the door. I looked through Varena's peephole. The knocker was a blond man, small, fair, with red-rimmed blue eyes. He looked mild and sad. I was sure I knew who it was.

"Emory Osborn," he said, when I opened the door. I shook his hand. His was that soft boneless handshake some men give a woman, as though they're scared if they squeeze with all their masculine power they'll break her delicate fingers. It felt like shaking hands with the Pillsbury Dough Boy. This was something Jess O'Shea and Emory Osborn had in common.

"Come in," I said. After all, he owned the cottage.

Emory Osborn stepped over the threshold. The widower was maybe 5′ 7″, not much taller than I. He was very fair and blue-eyed, handsome on a small scale, and he had the most flawless skin I'd ever seen on a man. Right at the moment, it was pink from the cold.

"I'm sorry for your loss," I told him.

He looked directly at me then. "You were here in the cottage last night?"

"Yes, I was."

"You saw her?"

"Yes."

"She was alive."

I shifted uneasily. "Yes," I told him reluctantly.

"Did she speak?"

"She asked after the children."

"The children?"

"That's all."

His eyes closed, and for one awful moment I thought he was going to cry.

"Have a seat," I said abruptly. I startled him into sitting down in the nearest chair, an armchair that must be Varena's favorite from the way she'd positioned it.

"Let me get you some hot chocolate." I went into the kitchen without waiting for an answer. I knew there would be some since Varena'd offered it to me the night before. There it was, on the counter where she'd set it, along with two mugs. Luckily, the microwave was built-in, so I was able to heat the water in it. I stirred in the powder. It wasn't very good, but it was hot and sweet, and he looked in need of both sugar and warmth.

"Where are the children?" I asked as I put his mug on the small oak table by the chair.

"They're with church members," he said. His voice was rich but not big.

"So, what can I do for you?" It didn't seem that he would say anything else unless I prompted him.

"I wanted to see where she died."

This was very nearly intolerable. "There, on the couch," I said brusquely.

He stared. "There aren't any stains," he told me.

"Varena slung a sheet over it." This was beyond strange. The back of my neck began to prickle. I wasn't going to sit knee to knee with him—I'd been perched on the ottoman that matched the chair—and point out where Meredith's head had been, what spot her feet had touched.

"Before your friend put Meredith down?"

"Yes." I jumped up to pull a fitted sheet from the closet. Giving way to an almost irresistible compulsion, I refolded it, and knew I'd straighten all the rest, too. The hell with Varena's finer feelings.

"And he is—?"

"My friend." I could hear my voice get flatter and harder.

"You're angry with me, I'm afraid," he said wearily. And sure enough, he was weeping, tears were running down his cheeks. He blotted them automatically with a well-used handkerchief.

"You shouldn't put yourself through this." My tone was still not the one a nice woman would use to a widower. I meant he shouldn't put *me* through it.

"I feel like God's abandoned me and the kids. I'm heart-broken," and I reflected I'd never actually heard anyone use that word out loud, "and my faith has left me," he finished, without taking a breath. He put his face in his hands.

Oh, man. I didn't want to hear this. I didn't want to be here.

Through the uncurtained window, I saw a car pull in behind mine in the cottage's narrow driveway. Jess O'Shea got out and began his way to the door, his head bowed. A minister—just the person to deal with a lapse of faith and recent bereavement. I opened the door before he had a chance to knock.

"Jess," I said. Even I could hear the naked relief in my voice. "Emory Osborn is here, and he is really, really . . ." I stood there, nodding significantly, unable to pin down exactly what Emory Osborn was.

Jess O'Shea seemed to be taking in my drift. He stepped around me and over to the smaller man, claiming my former seat on the ottoman. He took Emory's hands in his.

I tried to block out the two men's voices as I continued the job of packing, despite the feeling I should leave while Emory talked with his minister. But Emory had the option of going to his own house if he wanted complete privacy. If I looked at it practically, he'd known I was here and come in the cottage anyway . . .

Jess and Emory were praying together now, the fervent expression on Emory's face the only one I could see. Jess's back was bent and his hands clasped in front of his face. The two fair heads were close together.

Then Dill stepped in, looking at the two men praying, at me folding, trying to keep my eyes to myself. He looked startled and not too happy at this tableau.

All three dads in the same room. Except that one of them was probably not really a father at all but a thief who had stolen his fatherhood.

Dill turned to me, his whole face a question. I shrugged.

"Where's Varena?" he whispered.

"At our folks'," I whispered. "You go over there. You two need to talk about what's going to happen. And aren't you supposed to be meeting Jack at your place?" I gave him a little push with my hand, and he took a step back before he recovered his footing. Possibly I'd pushed a little harder than I'd planned.

After Dill obediently got in his car and left, I finished refolding and found I had packed all the remaining items in the linen closet. I checked the bathroom cabinet. It held only a few things, which I also boxed.

When I turned around, Jess O'Shea was right behind me. My arms tensed immediately and my hands fisted.

"Sorry, did I surprise you?" he asked, with apparent innocence.

"Yes."

"I think Emory is feeling a little better. We're going over to his house. Thanks for comforting him."

I couldn't recall any comforting I'd done; it must have been in the eye of the comfortee. I made a noncommittal sound.

"I'm so glad you've returned to reconcile with your family," Jess said, all in a rush. "I know this has meant so much to them."

This was his business? I raised my eyebrows.

He reddened when I didn't speak. "I guess it's a professional hazard, giving out emotional pats on the back," he said finally. "I apologize."

I nodded. "How is Krista?" I asked.

"She's fine," he said, surprised. "It's a little hard to get her to understand that her friend's mother is gone, she seems not to see it as a reality yet. That can be a blessing, you know.

119

I think we'll be keeping Eve for a while until Emory can cope a little better. Maybe the baby, too, if Lou thinks she can handle it."

"Didn't Lou tell me she'd taken Krista to the doctor last week?" I asked.

If Jess noticed the contrast between my lack of response to his observations about my family and my willingness to chatter about his child, he didn't comment on it. Parents almost always seem willing to believe other people are as fascinated with their children as they are.

"No," he said, obviously searching his memory. "Krista hasn't even had a cold since we started her on her allergy shots last summer." His face lightened. "Before that, we were in to Dr. LeMay's every week, it seemed like! My goodness, this is so much better. Lou gives Krista the shots herself."

I nodded and began opening cabinets in the kitchen. Jess took the hint and left, pulling on his heavy coat as he walked across the yard. Evidently he wasn't going to stay at Emory's long.

After he left I wrote a note on a pad I found under Varena's phone. I hopped in my car and drove to the motel. As I'd expected, Jack's car wasn't there. I pulled up in front of his room. I squatted and slid the note under his door.

It said, "Krista O'Shea didn't go to the doctor recently." I didn't sign it. Who else would be leaving Jack a note?

On my way back to Varena's, I scavenged alleys for more boxes. I was particularly interested in the alley behind the gift store and furniture store.

It was clean, for an alley, and I even scored a couple of very decent boxes before I began my search. There was a Dumpster back there; I was sure the police had been through it, since it was suspiciously empty. The appliance carton Christopher Sims had been using for shelter was gone, too, maybe appropriated by the police.

I looked down the alley in both directions. Main Street was on one end, and anyone driving east would be able to glance down the alley and catch a glimpse of whoever was in it, unless that person was in the niche where Sims's box had been located.

To the south end of the alley was a quiet street with small businesses in older houses and a few remaining homes still occupied by one family apiece. That street, Macon, saw quite a lot of foot traffic; the square's parking space was severely limited, so downtown shoppers were always looking for a spot within walking distance.

It sure would be easy to catch a glimpse of Christopher Darby Sims while he squatted in this alley. It sure would be tempting to capitalize on the presence of a homeless black in Bartley. It would be no trouble at all to slip through the alley with, say, a length of bloody pipe. Deposit it behind a handy box.

The back door of the furniture store opened. A woman about my age came out, looking cautiously at me.

"Hi," she called. She was clearly waiting for me to account for my presence.

"I'm collecting boxes for my sister's move," I told her, gesturing toward my car with its open trunk.

"Oh," she said, relief written on her face in big bold letters. "I hate to seem suspicious, but we had a . . . Lily?"

"Maude? Mary Maude?" I was looking at her just as incredulously.

She came down the back steps of the building in a rush and threw her arms around me. I staggered back under her weight. Mary Maude was still pretty and always would be, but she was considerably rounder than she had been in high school. I made myself hug her back. "Mary Maude Plummer," I said tentatively, patting her plump shoulder very gently.

"Well, it was Mary Maude Baumgartner for about five years, and now it's back to Plummer," she told me, sniffing a little. Mary Maude had always been emotional. I had a clenched feeling around my heart. I had a lot of memories of this woman.

"You never called me," she said now, looking up at me. She meant, after the rape. I could never get away from it here.

"I never called anyone," I said. I had to tell Mary Maude the truth. "I couldn't face doing it. I had too hard a time."

Her eyes filled with tears. "But I've always loved you."

Always right to the emotional truth, no matter how uncomfortable. Could this be why I'd never called Mary Maude after my Bad Time? We'd let go of each other, taken a step back.

I remembered another important truth. "I love you too," I said. "But I couldn't stand to be around people who were always thinking about what had happened to me. I couldn't do it."

She nodded. Her red hair, almost to her shoulders, turned under in a neat curve all the way around, and she had heavy gold earrings in her pierced ears. "I think I can understand that. I've been all these years forgiving you for refusing my comfort."

"Are we all right?"

"Yeah," she said, smiling up at me. "We're all right, now."

We both gave a little laugh, half happy, half embarrassed.

"So, you're getting boxes for Varena?"

"Yeah. She's getting her stuff out of the cottage. The wedding's day after tomorrow. And after the murder last night . . ."

"Oh, right, that's the place Varena rented! You know, the husband, Emory, works right here, with me." And Mary Maude pointed at the door from which she'd issued. "He's the sweetest guy."

He would certainly have been aware of Christopher Sims's presence in the alley in back of the store.

"So, I guess you knew this guy was living back here, the purse snatcher?"

"Well, we'd caught glimpses. Just in the two days before the police got him. Wait . . . my God, Lily, was that you who kicked him?"

I nodded.

"Wow, girl, what have you done with yourself?" She eyed me up and down.

"Taken karate for a few years, worked out some."

"I can tell! You were so brave, too!"

"So you knew Sims was back here?"

"Huh? Oh, yeah. But we weren't sure what to do about it. We've never had any problem like that, and we were trying to decide what the safe thing to do was, and what the Christian thing to do was. It's tough when that might not be the same thing! We got Jess O'Shea down here to talk to the man, try to see where he wanted a bus ticket to, you know? Or if he was sick. Or hungry."

So Jess had actually met the man.

"What did Jess say?"

"He said this Sims guy told him he was just fine right where he was, he had been getting handouts from some people in the, you know, black community, and he was just going to stay in the alley until God guided him somewhere else."

"Somewhere where they had more purses?"

"Could be." Mary Maude laughed. "I hear Diane positively identified him. He told Diane at the police station that he was an angel and was trying to point out to Diane the hazards of possessing too many worldly goods."

"That's original."

"Yeah, give him points for a talent for fiction, anyway."

"He say anything about the murders?" Since Mary Maude apparently had such access to the local gossip pipeline, I thought I might as well tap in.

"No. Isn't that a little strange? You'd think on one hand he'd be too deranged to understand that the murders are so much more serious, and yet he's saying that he never saw the pipe until the police found it stuffed behind his box, you know, the one where he was sleeping."

I noticed that Mary Maude had come to check me out without a coat on, and she was shivering in her expensive white blouse and sweater-vest embroidered in holly and Christmas ornaments. Our reunion had its own background sound track, as the loudspeakers positioned around the square continued to blare out Christmas music.

"How do you stand it?" I asked, nodding my head toward the noise in the square.

"The carols? Oh, after a while you just tune them out," she said wearily. "They just leach the spirit out of me."

"Maybe that's what made the purse snatcher deranged,"

I offered, and she burst into laughter. Mary Maude had always laughed easily, charmingly, making it impossible not at least to smile along with her.

She hugged me again, made me promise to call her when I came back to town after the wedding, and scampered back into the store, her body shaking with the cold. I stood looking after her for a minute. Then I threw a couple more boxes into the car and drove carefully out of the alley.

Within a block of turning out onto the side street, Macon, I passed Dill's pharmacy.

I had a lot to think about.

I would have given almost anything to have had my punching bag.

I returned to Varena's place and packed everything I could find. Every half hour or so, I straightened up and looked out the window. There were lots of visitors at the Osborn house: women dropping off food, mostly. Emory appeared in the yard from time to time, walking restlessly, and a couple of times he was crying. Once he drove off in his car, returning in less than an hour. But he didn't knock on the cottage door again, to my great relief.

I had carefully folded Varena's remaining clothes and placed them in suitcases, since I didn't know what she'd planned on taking on the honeymoon. Most of her clothes were already at Dill's.

Finally, by three o'clock, all Varena's belongings were packed. I moved all the boxes into my car, except for a short stack by the front door that just couldn't fit. And of course, there was the remaining furniture, but that wasn't my problem.

I began cleaning the apartment.

It felt surprisingly good to have something to clean. Varena, while not a slob, was no compulsive housekeeper, and there was plenty to do. I was also actively enjoying the break from my family and the alone time.

As I was running the vacuum, I heard a heavy knock on the door. I jumped. I hadn't heard a car pull up, but then I wouldn't have over the drone of the machine.

I opened the door. Jack was there, and he was angry.

"What?" I asked.

He pushed past me. "My room at the motel got broken into." He was furious. "Someone came in through the bathroom window. It looks out on a field. No one saw."

"Anything taken?"

"No. Whoever it was rummaged through everything, broke the lock on my briefcase."

I had an ominous sinking somewhere in the region of my stomach. "Did you find my note?"

"What?" He stared at me, anger giving way to something else.

"I left you a note." I sat down abruptly on the ottoman. "I left you a note," I repeated stupidly. "About Krista O'Shea."

"You signed it?"

"No."

"What did it say?"

"That she hadn't been to the doctor in weeks."

Jack's eyes flickered from item to item in the clean room, as he thought about what I'd told him.

"Did you call the police?" I asked.

"They were there when I pulled in. Mr. Patel, the manager, had called. He had seen the window was broken when he went to put the garbage out behind the building."

"What did you tell them?"

"The truth. That my things had been gone through but nothing had been stolen. I hadn't left any money in my room. I never do. And I don't carry valuable things with me."

Jack felt angry and sick because his space, however temporary, had been invaded, and his things had been riffled. I understand that feeling all too well. But Jack would never talk about it in those terms, because he was a man.

"So now someone knows exactly why I'm here in Bartley." He'd cover that violated feeling with practical considerations.

"That person also knows I have an accomplice," he continued.

That was one way to put it.

Suddenly I stood, walked over to the window. I was crackling with restless energy. Trouble was coming, and every nerve in my body was warning me to get in my car and go home to Shakespeare.

But *I couldn't go.* My *family* kept me here.

No, that wasn't completely true. I could have brought myself to leave my family if I felt threatened enough. *Jack* kept me here.

Without a thought in my head, I made a fist and would have driven it into the window if Jack hadn't caught my arm.

I rounded on him, crazy with jolts of feeling that I wouldn't identify. Instead of striking him, I ran my arm around his neck and drew him ferociously to me. The stresses and strains on me were almost intolerable.

Jack, understandably surprised, made a questioning noise but then shut up. He let go of the arm he was gripping and tentatively put his own arms around me. We stood silently for what seemed like a long time.

"So," he said, "you want to talk about whatever this is that's got you so upset? Have you run out of tolerance for being in your parents' house? Has your sister made you mad? Or . . . have you found out something else about her fiancé?"

I pushed away from him and began to pace the room.

"I have some ideas," I said.

His dark brows flew up. I should've kept my mouth shut. I didn't want to have the whole conversation: I'd tell him I would get in the houses, he'd tell me it was his job, blah blah blah. Why not skip the whole thing?

"Lily, I'm going to get mad at you," Jack said with a sort of fatalistic certainty.

"You can't do the things I can do. What's your next step now?" I challenged him. "Is there one more thing you can find out here?"

Sure enough, he was looking angry already. He stuck his hands in the pockets of his leather jacket and glanced around for something handy to kick. Finding nothing, he too began pacing. We shifted around the room as if we were sword fighters waiting for our opponent to give us an opening.

"Ask the chief if I can go in and look at those files at Dr. LeMay's," he suggested defiantly.

"It'll never happen." I knew Chandler: He would go only so far.

"Find whatever the murderer was wearing when he killed the doctor and the nurse and Meredith Osborn."

So Jack had decided, as I had, that the killer had worn some covering garment over his clothes.

"It's not gonna be in the house," I told him.

"You think not?"

"I know not. When people hide something like that, they want it to be close but not as personally close as their own house."

"You're thinking carport, garage?"

I nodded. "Or car. But you know as well as I do that'll put you in a terrible position legally. Before you do that, isn't there anything else you can try?"

"I'd hoped to get something from Dill. He's a nice guy, but he just won't talk about his first marriage. At least his attic has a good floored section now." Jack gave a short laugh. "I thought about going back to reinterview the couple that lived next door to Meredith and Emory when they had their first child," Jack said reluctantly. "I've been reviewing what they said, and I think I see a hole in their account."

"Where do they live?"

"The podunk town north of Little Rock where the Osborns lived before they came here. You know . . . the one not far from Conway."

"What was the hole?"

"Not so much a hole, as . . . something the woman said just didn't make sense. She said that Meredith told her the baby coming was the saddest day of her life. And Meredith told her that the home birth had been terrible."

That could be significant or just plain nothing more than what it was, the outpourings of a woman who'd just experienced childbirth for the first time.

"She had the second baby in the hospital," I observed. "At least, I assume so; I think someone would have mentioned it before now if she'd had Jane Lilith at home." But I made a mental note to check.

"Why would Meredith have to die?" Jack said. "Why Meredith?" He wasn't talking to me, not really. He was staring out the front window, his hands still in his pockets. Seen in profile, he looked stern and frightening. If I mentally lopped off his ponytail, I could see how he'd looked as a cop. I would not have been afraid of being beaten if I'd been arrested by him, I thought, but I would have known I'd be a fool to try to escape.

"She baby-sat the other two girls," I offered.

Jack nodded. "So she knew them all physically. She'd have an opportunity, sooner or later, to see each girl naked. But the Macklesby baby didn't have any distinguishing physical marks."

"So who do you think sent you the picture?"

"I think it was Meredith Osborn." He turned from the window to look at me directly. "I think she sent it because she wanted to right some great wrong. And I think that's why she was killed."

"What were you really doing the night she died?"

"I was on my way to ask her some questions," he said. "I'd driven past the Bartley Grill, and I saw her husband and the kids inside. The baby was on the table in one of those carriers, and he and Eve were chattering away. So I knew Meredith was home by herself, and I thought she might know more about the picture."

"Why?"

"Roy had brushed the picture and the envelope for fingerprints. There weren't any on the picture—it had been wiped—but there was one on the envelope, on the tape used to seal the flap. It was a clear print, very small. You'd told me how little Meredith was. Did you ever notice how tiny her hands were?"

130

I never had.

"I'd hoped to get some fingerprints of hers to compare. I planned on ringing the doorbell, telling her that I was a detective in town on a job as well as being your boyfriend. I was going to hand her a photo, ask her to identify it. When she said she didn't know the subject, I would put the photo in a bag and later test it for fingerprints."

If I were in the Osborn house I could find something I could almost bet would have her fingerprints on it. I could also check to see if Eve's memory book was missing a page.

"But I don't want you getting into this. You saw how she died," Jack said brutally. I looked up sharply. He was standing right in front of me.

"I can tell when you're going to do something; you get this stubborn clench to your jaw," he continued. "What's in your head, Lily?"

"Cleaning," I said.

"Cleaning what?"

"Cleaning the Osborn house, and the Kingery house."

He thought that over. "This isn't your case," he said.

"I want us out of here by Christmas."

"Me too," he said fervently.

"Well, then," I said, concluding our discussion.

"Did I just say something I didn't know I said?"

"We agree on getting this done by Christmas."

Jack gave me a dark look. "So, I'm driving out of here," he said abruptly. "I'll call you. Don't do anything that could put you in danger."

"Drive careful," I told him. He gave me an unloving peck on the cheek, another suspicious look, and, without further ado, he left. I watched through the uncurtained window as Jack fastened his seat belt and backed out of the driveway.

Then I went over to the widower and offered to clean his house.

SIX

Since Emory was so fine-boned and fair, the swollen red eyes made him look rabbity. Those eyes hardly seemed to register my identity. He was completely preoccupied, eaten up from the inside out.

"Ah, yes? What can I do for you?" he asked me, his voice coming from a great interior distance.

"I've come to clean your house."

"What?"

"That's what I do for a living, clean. This is what I can offer you in your time of trouble."

He was still bewildered. I was unhappy with myself, so it was more difficult to keep my impatience under wraps.

"My sister . . ." he faltered. "She'll be coming tomorrow."

"Then you need the house clean for her arrival."

He stared some more. I stared right back. Behind him,

down a dark hall, I saw Eve creep out of an open doorway. She looked like a little ghost of herself.

"Miss Lily," she said. "Thanks for coming."

It was what she'd heard her father say to callers all day, and her attempt to be adult gave my heart a little pang. I also wondered what Eve was doing at home, when I'd thought she was with the O'Sheas.

Emory finally stood aside so I could enter, but he still seemed uncertain. I glanced at my watch, letting him know how valuable I thought my time was, and that shook him from his lethargy.

"This is so kind of you, Miss . . . Bard," he said. "Is there anything we need to . . . ?"

"I expect Eve can show me where things are." I am no grief counselor. I don't know squat about children. But it's always better to be busy.

"That would be good," Emory said vaguely. "So I'll . . ." and he just wandered off. "Oh, Eve," he said over his shoulder, "remember your company manners. Stay with Miss Bard."

Eve looked a little resentful, but she replied, "Yes, Daddy."

The girl and I looked at each other carefully. "Where's the baby?" I asked.

"She's at the O'Sheas' house. I was there for a while, too, but Daddy said I needed to come home."

"All right, then. Where is the kitchen?"

Her lips curved in an incredulous smile. Surely everyone knew where the kitchen was! But Eve was polite, and she guided me to the back of the house and to the right.

"Where's all the cleaning stuff?" I asked. I set my purse

down on the kitchen counter, shrugged off my coat, and hung it on one of the kitchen chairs.

Eve opened a cupboard in the adjacent washroom. I could see that the laundry basket was full of clothes.

"Maybe you better show me the house before I start."

So the little girl showed me her home. It was a large older house, with high ceilings and dark hardwood paneling and floors that needed work. I noticed the register of a floor furnace. I hadn't seen one of those in years. A Christmas tree decorated with religious symbols stood in the living room, the family's only communal room. The sofa, coffee table, and chair combo was maple with upholstery of a muted brown plaid. Clean but hideous.

Emory was slumped in the chair, his hand wrapped around a cold mug that had held coffee. I knew it was cold because I could see the ring around the middle. He'd had a drink after it had been sitting a spell. He didn't acknowledge our passage through the room. I wondered if I'd have to dust him like a piece of furniture.

The master bedroom was tidy, but the furniture needed polishing. Eve's room . . . well, her bed had been made haphazardly, but the floor was littered with Barbies and coloring books. The baby's room was neatest, since the baby couldn't walk yet. The diaper pail needed emptying. The bathroom needed a complete scrubbing. The kitchen was not too bad.

"Where are the sheets?" I asked.

Eve said, "Mama's are in there." She pointed to the double closet in the master bedroom.

I stripped down the double bed, carried the dirty sheets to the washroom, started a load of wash. Back in the bedroom, I opened the closet door.

"There's Mama's stool," Eve said helpfully. "She always needs it to get things down from the closet shelf."

I was at least six inches taller than Meredith Osborn had been, and I could easily reach the shelf. But if I wanted to look at what was behind the sheets, the stool would be handy.

I stepped up, lifted the set of sheets, and scanned the contents of the closet shelf. Another blanket for the bed, a box marked "Shoe Polish," a cheap metal box for files and important papers. Then, under a pile of purses, I spotted a box marked "Eve." After I'd snapped the clean sheets on the bed, I sent Eve out of the room to fetch a dustcloth and the furniture polish.

I lifted down the box and opened it. I had to clench my teeth to make myself examine its contents. My sense of invasion was overwhelming.

In the box were faded "Welcome, Baby" cards, the kind family and friends send a couple when they have a child. I quickly riffled through them. They were only what they seemed. Also in the box was a little rattle and a baby outfit. It was soft knit, yellow, with little green giraffes scattered over it, the usual snap crotch and long sleeves. It had been folded carefully. Eve's coming home from the hospital outfit, maybe. But Eve had been born at home, I remembered. Well, then, Meredith's favorite of all Eve's baby clothes. My mother had some of mine and Varena's still packed away in our attic.

I closed the box and popped it back into position. By the time Eve returned, I had the flowered bedspread smoothed flat and taut across the bed and the blanket folded at the foot.

Together, we polished and dusted. Eve naturally didn't do things the most efficient way, since she was a grieving eight-year-old child. I am rigid about the way I like housework done and not used to working with anyone, but I managed it.

I'd had a pang of worry about Eve handling her mother's belongings, but Eve seemed to do that so matter-of-factly that I wondered if she didn't yet comprehend that her mother would not be returning.

In the course of cleaning that room I made sure I examined every nook and cranny. Short of going through the chest of drawers and the drawers in the night tables, I saw what there was to see in that bedroom: under the bed, the corners of the closet, the backs and bottoms of almost every single piece of furniture. Later, when I began to put the laundry away, I even caught glimpses of what was in the drawers. Just the usual stuff, as far as I could tell.

One drawer of the little desk in the corner was stacked with medical bills related to Meredith's pregnancy. At a glance, it had been a difficult one. I hoped the furniture store had a group policy.

"Shake the can, Eve," I reminded her, and she shook the yellow aerosol can of furniture polish. "Now, spray."

She carefully sent a stream of polish onto the bare top of the desk. I swabbed with a cloth, over and over, then put the letter rack, mug full of pens and pencils, and box containing stamps and return address labels back in their former positions. When Eve excused herself to use the bathroom, I gritted my teeth and did something that disgusted me: I picked up Meredith Osborn's hairbrush, which could reasonably be assumed to have her fingerprints on it, wrapped it in a discarded plastic cleaner's bag, and stepped through to the kitchen and shoved it in my purse.

I was back in the Osborns' bedroom, tamping the stack of papers so the edges were square and neat, when Eve came back.

"Those are Mama's bills," she said importantly. "We always pay our bills."

"Of course." I gathered the cleaning things and handed some of them to Eve. "We've finished here."

As we began to work on Eve's room, I could tell that the little girl was getting bored, after the novelty of helping me work wore thin.

"Where'd you eat last night?" I asked casually.

"We went to the restaurant," she said. "I got a milkshake. Jane slept the whole time. It was great."

"Your dad was with you," I observed.

"Yeah, he wanted to give Mama a night off," Eve said approvingly. Then the ending of that night off hit her in the face, and I saw her pleasure in the little memory of the milkshake crumple. I could not ask her any more questions about last night.

"Why don't you find your last school memory book and show me who your friends are?" I suggested, as I got her clean sheets out of her little closet and began to remake her single bed.

"Oh, sure!" Eve said enthusiastically. She began to rummage through the low bookcase that was filled with children's books and knickknacks. Nothing in the bookcase seemed to be in any particular order, and I wasn't too surprised when Eve told me she couldn't come up with her most recent memory book. She fetched one from two years ago instead and had an excellent time telling me the name of every child in every picture. I was required only to smile and nod, and every now and then I said, "Really?" As casually as I could manage it, I went through the books in the bookcase myself. The past year's memory book wasn't there.

Eve relaxed perceptibly as she looked at the pictures of her friends and acquaintances.

"Did you go to the doctor last week, Eve?" I asked casually.

"Why do you want to know that?" she asked.

I was floored. It hadn't occurred to me that a child would ask me why I wanted to know.

"I just wondered what doctor you went to."

"Doctor LeMay." Her brown eyes looked huge as she thought about her answer. "He's dead, too," she said wearily, as if the whole world was dying around her. To Eve, it must have felt so.

I could not think of a natural, painless way to ask again, and I just couldn't put the girl through any more grief. To my surprise, Eve volunteered, "Mama went with me."

"She did?" I tried to keep my voice as noncommittal as possible.

"Yep. She liked Dr. LeMay, Miss Binnie, too."

I nodded, lifting a stack of coloring books and shaking them into an orderly rectangle.

"It hurt, but it was over before too long," Eve said, obviously quoting someone.

"What was over?" I asked.

"They took my blood," Eve said importantly.

"Yuck."

"Yeah, it hurt," said the girl, shaking her head just like a middle-aged woman, philosophically. "But some things hurt, and you just gotta handle it."

I nodded. This was a lot of stoical philosophy from a third grader.

"I was losing weight, and my mama thought something might be wrong," Eve explained.

"So, what was wrong?"

"I don't know." Eve looked down at her feet. "She never said."

I nodded as if that were quite usual. But what Eve had told me worried me, worried me badly. What if something really was wrong physically with the child? Surely her father knew about it, about the visit and the blood test? What if Eve were anemic or had some worse disease?

She looked healthy enough to me, but I was certainly willing to concede that I was hardly a competent judge. Eve was thin and pale, yes, but not abnormally so. Her hair shone and her teeth looked sound and clean, she smelled good and she stood like she was comfortable, and she was able to meet my eyes: The absence of any of these conditions is reason to worry, their presence reassuring. So why wasn't I relaxing?

We moved on to the baby's room, Eve shadowing my every step. From time to time the doorbell rang, and I would hear Emory drift through the house to answer it, but the callers never stayed long. Faced with Emory's naked grief, it would be hard to stand and chat.

After I'd finished the baby's room and the bathroom, I entered the kitchen to find that food was accumulating faster than Emory could store it. He was standing there with a plastic bowl in his hands, a bowl wrapped in the rose-colored plastic wrap that was so popular locally. I opened the refrigerator and evaluated the situation.

"Hmmm," I said. I began removing everything. Emory put the bowl down and helped. All the little odds and ends of leftovers went into the garbage, the dishes they'd been in went in the sink, and I wiped down the bottom shelf where there'd been a little spillage.

"Do you have a list?" I asked Emory.

He seemed to come out of his trance. "A list?" he asked, as if he'd never heard the word.

"You need to keep a list of who brings what food in what dish. Do you have a piece of paper handy?" That sister of Emory's needed to get here fast.

"Daddy, I've got notebook paper in my room!" Eve said and ran off to fetch it.

"I guess I knew that, but I forgot," Emory said. He blinked his red eyes, seemed to wake up a little. When Eve dashed into the kitchen with several sheets of paper, he hugged her. She wriggled in his grasp.

"We have to start the list, Daddy!" She looked up at him sternly.

I thought that Eve had probably been hugged and patted enough for two lifetimes in the day just past.

She began the list herself, in shaky and idiosyncratic writing. I told her how to do it, and she perched on a stool at the counter, laboriously entering the food gifts on one side, the bringer on the other, and a star when there was a dish that had to be returned.

Galvanized by our activity, Emory began making calls from the telephone on the kitchen counter. I gathered from the snatches of conversation I overheard that he was calling the police department to find out when they thought Meredith's body could come back from its autopsy in Little Rock, making arrangements for the music at the funeral service, checking in at work, trying to start his life back into motion. He began writing his own list, in tiny, illegible writing. It was a list of things to do before the funeral, he told me in his quiet voice. I was glad to see him shake off his torpor.

It was getting late so I accelerated my work rate, sweeping and mopping and wiping down the kitchen counters with dispatch. I selected a few dishes for Emory and Eve's supper, leaving them on the counter with heating instructions. Emory was still talking on the phone, so I just drifted out of the room with Eve behind me. I pulled on my coat, pulled up the strap of the purse.

"Can you come back, Lily?" Eve asked. "You know how to do everything."

I looked down at her. I was betraying this child and her father, abusing their trust. Eve's admiration for me was painful.

"I can't come back tomorrow, no," I said as gently as I was capable of. "Varena's getting married the day after, and I still have a lot to do for that. But I'll try to see you again."

"OK." She took that in a soldierlike way, which I was beginning to understand was typical of Eve Osborn. "And thank you for helping today," Eve said, after a couple of gulps. Very much woman of the house.

"I figured cleaning would be more use than more food."

"You were right," she said soberly. "The house looks so much nicer."

"See ya," I said. I bent to give her a little hug. I felt awkward. "Take care of yourself." What a stupid thing to tell a child, I castigated myself, but I had no idea what else to say.

Emory was standing by the front door. I felt like snarling. I had almost made it out without talking to him. "I can't thank you enough for this," he said, his sincerity painful and unwelcome.

"It was nothing."

"No, no," he insisted. "It meant so much to us." He was going to cry again.

Oh, hell. "Good-bye," I told him firmly and was out the door.

Glancing down at my watch again as I walked out to my car, I realized there was no way to get out of explaining to my folks where I'd been and what I'd been doing.

To compound my guilt, my parents thought I'd done a wonderful Christian thing, helping out Emory Osborn in his hour of travail. I had to let them think the best of me when I least deserved it.

I tried hard to pack my guilt into a smaller space in my heart. Reduced to the most basic terms, the Osborns now had a clean house in which to receive visitors. And I had a negative report for Jack. I hadn't discovered anything of note, except for Eve's trip to the doctor. Though I had stolen the brush.

When Varena emerged from her room, looking almost as weepy as Emory, I put the second part of my plan into effect.

"I'm in the cleaning mood," I told her. "How about me cleaning Dill's house, so it'll be nice for your first Christmas together?" Varena and Dill weren't leaving for their honeymoon until after Christmas, so they'd be together at home with Anna.

Somehow, since my mission was to save Varena grief, I didn't feel quite as guilty as I had when I'd told Emory I was going to clean his house. But I had a sour taste in my mouth, and I figured it was self-disgust.

"Thanks," Varena said, surprise evident in her voice. "That would really be a load off my mind. You're sure?"

"You know I need something to do," I told her truthfully.

"Bless your heart," Varena said with compassion, giving me a hug. Somehow, my sister's unwanted sympathy stiffened my resolve.

Then the doorbell rang, and it was some friends of my parents', just back from a trip to see the Christmas decorations at Pigeon Forge. They were full of their trip and had brought a present for Dill and Varena. It was easy for me to slip off to my room after a proper greeting. I took a hot, hot shower and waited for Jack to call me.

He didn't. The phone rang off the wall that evening, the callers ranging from friends wanting to check on wedding plans, Dill asking for Varena, credit card companies wanting to extend new cards to my parents, and church members trying to arrange a meal for the Osborn family after the relatives had arrived for Meredith's funeral.

But no Jack.

Something was niggling at me, and I wanted to look at the pictures of Summer Dawn at eight. I wanted to ask Jack some questions. I wanted to look at his briefcase. That was the closest I could get to figuring out what was bothering me.

About eight-thirty, I called Chandler McAdoo. "Let's go riding," I said.

Chandler pulled into my parents' drive in his own vehicle, a Jeep. He was wearing a heavy red-and-white-plaid flannel shirt, a camo jacket, jeans, and Nikes.

My mother answered the door before I could get there.

"Chandler," she said, sounding a little at sea. "Did you need to ask us something about the other day?"

"No, ma'am. I'm here to pick up Lily." He was wearing an Arkansas Travellers gimme cap, and the bill of it tilted as he nodded at me. I was pulling on my coat.

"*This* brings back old times," my mother said with a smile.

"See you in a while, Mom," I said, zipping up my old red Squall jacket.

"Okay, sweetie. You two have a good time."

I liked the Jeep. Chandler kept it spick-and-span, and I approved. Jack tended to distribute paperwork all over his car.

"So, where we going?" Chandler asked.

"It's too cold and we're too old for Frankel's Pond," I said. "What about the Heart of the Delta?"

"The Heart it is," he said.

By the time we scooted into a booth at the home-owned diner we'd patronized all through high school, I was in the midst of being updated about Chandler's two stabs at marriage, the little boy he was so proud of (by Cindy, wife number two), and the current woman in his life—Tootsie Monahan, my least favorite of Varena's bridesmaids.

When we had glanced at the menu—which seemed almost eerily the same as it had been when I was sixteen, except for the prices—and had given the waitress our order (a hamburger with everything and fries for Chandler, a butterscotch milkshake for me), Chandler gave me a sharp, let's-get-down-to-it look.

"So what's the deal with this guy you've hooked up with?"

"Jack."

"I know his damn name. What's his business here?"

Chandler and I stared at each other for a moment. I took a deep breath.

"He's tracing an . . ." I stopped dead. How could I do this? Where did my loyalty lie?

Chandler made a rotary movement with his hand, wanting me to spill it out.

Chandler had already told Jack several things, operating on his affection for me. But the actual physical effort of opening my mouth, telling him Jack's business, was almost impossible. I closed my eyes for a second, took a deep breath. "A missing person," I said.

He absorbed that.

"Okay, tell me."

I hesitated. "It's not my call."

"What do you want from me, Lily?"

Chandler's face was infinitely older.

Oh, Jesus, I hated this.

"Tell me what people were doing when Meredith Osborn was killed. I don't know if that has anything to do with Jack's job, Chandler, and that's the truth. I was in that house, just a few feet away from her, and if there's anything I know it's how to fight." I hadn't known how that bothered me until I said it. "I didn't have a chance to lift a finger to help her. Just tell me about that evening."

He could do that without violating any laws, I figured.

"What people were doing. What happened to Meredith." Chandler appeared to be thinking, his eyes focused on the saltshaker with its grains of rice showing yellower than the stark white of the salt.

I didn't know I'd been holding my breath until Chandler began talking. He folded his small hands in front of him, and his face took on a faintly stern, stiff set that I realized must be his professional demeanor.

"Mrs. Osborn died, as far as I could tell by a visual exam, from multiple stab wounds to the chest," he began. "She'd been hit in the face, maybe to knock her on the ground so the stabbing would be easier. The attack took place in the backyard. It would have required only a minute or two. She wasn't able to move more than a yard after she was stabbed. Her wounds were very severe. Plus, the temperature was below freezing, and she didn't have a coat on."

"But she did move that one yard."

"Yes."

"Toward Varena's little house."

"Yes."

I could feel my mouth compress in a hard line and my eyes narrow, in what my friend Marshall had once called my "fist face."

"What kind of knife?"

"Some kind of single-blade kitchen knife, looked like, but we have to wait on the autopsy to be sure. We haven't found any kind of knife."

"Did you go in the Osborns' house?"

"Sure. We had to see if the killer was in there, and the back door was unlocked."

"So someone had made a noise, or called Meredith out of the house . . . ?"

He shrugged. "Something like that, we figure. She wasn't scared. She would have stayed in the house and locked the back door if she'd been scared. She could have called us. The phone was working, I checked. Instead, she went outside."

Unspoken between us lay the inescapable conclusion that Meredith had seen someone she knew and trusted in the yard.

"When does Emory say he left the house?"

"About seven. He had the two little girls. He wanted to give his wife some time to herself, he said. She'd had a hard time with the baby's birth, wasn't getting her strength back, and so on."

I raised my brows.

"Yes, the waitress confirms that Emory got to the restaurant about five after. It took about forty-five minutes for Emory and Eve to eat, and then the baby woke up and Emory gave her a bottle, burped her, the whole nine yards. So they left the restaurant maybe fifteen minutes after eight. Emory had some things to pick up at the Kmart, so he took the girls with him in there, and they got some vitamins and other junk . . . that brings us up to around eight-fifty, nine o'clock, somewhere in there."

"Then he comes home."

"Then he comes home," Chandler agreed. "He was mighty tore up. Turned white as a sheet."

"You had already searched the house?"

"Yes, had to. Didn't find any evidence anyone but the family had been in it. Nothing suspicious in any way. No forced entry, no threatening messages in the answering machine, no sign of a struggle . . . a big zero."

"Chandler . . ." I hesitated. But I could think of no other way to find out. "Did you search his car?"

Chandler shifted in his seat. "No. Do you think we should have?"

"Did you ask Eve if her dad had stopped back by the house for anything?"

"I did my best to ask her that. I had to be real careful how I put it, didn't want the girl to think we figured her dad had done it. She's just eight!" Chandler looked at me angrily, as if that were my doing.

"What did she say?" I asked, keeping my voice very quiet and level.

"She said they went to the restaurant. Period. Then to Kmart. Period."

I nodded, looked away. "Where was Jess O'Shea?" I asked.

I could feel the heat of Chandler's glare even though I was looking over at the chipped Formica counter.

"Dave asked Emory what church he went to, and when he said Presbyterian, we called Jess," Chandler said slowly. "Lou said he was over in his office counseling a member of the congregation."

"Did you call over there?"

"Yes."

"Get an answer?"

"Yes. But he said he couldn't come right that second."

I wondered if Jess had actually come over to the Osborns' house that night. I couldn't remember if the scene between him and Emory the next day had given me a sense of an original encounter or a continuation of a dialogue begun the night before. I had been so embarrassed that I had tried to block out their conversation.

"Did he give a reason?"

"I just assumed he had to finish talking to whoever was there."

The upshot was, Jess had been away from home and the

149

police had not asked him to account for his time. There was no reason why they should, from their point of view.

Varena had told me Dill was going to spend the evening at home with Anna. I didn't think Dill was the kind of father who'd leave Anna in the house by herself, but he could have worked it out somehow, I guessed. I wondered if I could think of a way to ask questions that wouldn't make red flags go up in Varena's mind.

"Lily, if someone's safety is at stake, or if you have any idea at all who killed that poor woman, you are legally obliged to tell me. Morally, too."

I looked into Chandler's round brown eyes. I'd known this man my whole life, been friends with him, off and on, that long. When I'd come home to Bartley after my spectacular victimization and subsequent media bath, Chandler had been a constant visitor. He'd been between marriages, and we had gone out to eat together, ridden around together, spent time together so I could get away from my family and their love that was just choking me.

During that time, seven years ago, we had also shared a horribly embarrassing evening in the big pickup Chandler had been driving then. But I was sure we both did our best not to remember that.

"I don't know the identity of anyone who is in danger," I said carefully. "I don't know who killed Meredith." That was absolutely true.

"You should tell me everything you know," Chandler said, his voice so low and intent it was as scary as a snake's rattle.

My hands, resting on the worn gray and pink Formica of the table's surface, clenched into hard fists. My heels dug into the wooden base of the booth, giving me launching power. A startled look crossed Chandler's face, and he leaned away from me.

"What's in your mind?" he asked sharply, and he brushed his empty plate to one side without taking his eyes off me, clearing his own deck for action.

For once, I was anxious to explain myself. But I couldn't. I took a couple of deep breaths, made myself relax.

"You love this man," he said.

I started to shake my head side to side: no. But I said, "Yes."

"This is the one."

I nodded, a jerky little up-and-down movement.

"And he doesn't . . . he can handle . . . what happened to you?"

"He doesn't mind the scars," I said, my voice as light and smooth as the changing scenery of a dream.

Chandler turned red. His eyes left mine, focused on the pattern of the Formica.

"It's OK," I told him, just above a whisper.

"Does he . . . does he know how lucky he is?" Chandler asked, not able to think of any other way of asking me if Jack loved me back.

"I don't know."

"Lily, if you want me to have a serious talk with this joker, just say the word." And he really meant it. I looked at Chandler with new eyes. This man would put himself through a humiliating conversation and not think twice about it.

"Will you make him go down on one knee and swear to forsake all others?" I was smiling a little, I couldn't help it.

"Damn straight."

This, too, he meant.

"What a great guy you are," I said. All the aggression leaked out of me, as if I was a balloon with a pinhole. "You've been talking with Jack, haven't you?"

"He's an ex-cop, and no matter how his career ended," and Chandler flushed uncomfortably since Jack had not exactly left the Memphis police force under creditable circumstances, "Jack Leeds was a good detective and made some good arrests. I called the Memphis cops, talked to a friend of mine there, as soon as I realized who he was."

That was interesting. Chandler had known Jack was in town probably before I did—and had checked up on him.

"Fact is, the only thing this guy knew against Jack was that he'd hooked up with a shady cleaning lady," Chandler said with a grin.

I grinned back. All the tension was gone, and we were old friends together. Without asking, Chandler paid for my milkshake and his meal, and I slid out of the booth and into my coat.

When he dropped me off at home, Chandler gave me a kiss on the cheek. We hadn't said another word about Meredith Osborn, or Dr. LeMay, or Jack. I knew Chandler had backed off only because he owed me, on some level: The last time we'd been together had been a terrible evening for both of us. Whatever the reason, I was grateful. But I knew that if Chandler thought I was concealing something that would contribute to solving the murders that had taken place in the town he was sworn to protect, he would come down on me like a ton of bricks.

We might be old friends, but we were both weighted down with adult burdens.

. . .

Jack didn't call.

That night I lay sleepless, my arms rigidly at my sides, watching the bars of moonlight striping the ceiling of my old room. It was the distillation of the all the bad nights I'd had in the past seven years; except in my parents' house, I could not resort to my usual methods of escape and relief. Finally I got up, sat in the little slipper chair in the corner of the room, and turned on the lamp.

I'd finished my biography. Luckily I'd brought some paperbacks with me from Varena's, anticipating just such a night . . . not that I would have picked these books if I'd had much choice. The first was a book of advice on dealing with your stepchildren, and the second was a historical romance. Its cover featured a guy with an amazing physique. I stared at his bare, hairless chest with its immense pectorals, wondering if even my sensei's musculature would match this man's. I found it very unlikely that a sensible fighting man would wear his shirt halfway off his shoulders in that inconvenient and impractical way, and I thought it even sillier that his lady friend would choose to try to embrace him when he was leaning down from a horse. I calculated his weight, the angle of his upper body, and the pull she was exerting. I factored in the high wind blowing her hair out in a fan, and decided Lord Robert Dumaury was going to end up on the ground at Phillipetta Dunmore's feet within seconds, probably dislocating his shoulder in the process . . . and that's if he was lucky. I shook my head.

So I plowed through the advice, learning more about being a new mother to a growing not-your-own child than I ever wanted to know. This paperback showed serious signs of being read and reread. I hoped it would be of more use to Varena than Ms. Dunmore's adventures with Pectoral Man.

I would have given anything for a good thick biography.

I got halfway through the book before sleep overcame me. I was still in the chair, the lamp still on, when I woke at seven to the sounds of my family stirring.

I felt exhausted, almost too tired to move.

I did some push-ups, tried some leg lifts. But my muscles felt slack and weak, as if I were recovering from major surgery. Slowly, I pulled on my sweats. I'd committed my morning to cleaning Dill's house. But instead of rising and getting into the bathroom, I sat back in the chair with my face covered by my hands.

Being involved in this child abduction felt so wrong, so bad, but for my family's sake I couldn't imagine what else I could do. With a sigh of sheer weariness, I hauled myself to my feet and opened the bedroom door to reenter my family's life.

It was like dipping your toes into a quiet pond, only to have a whirlpool suck you under.

Since this was the day before the wedding, Mother and Varena had every hour mapped out. Mother had to go to the local seamstress's house to pick up the dress she planned to wear tomorrow: It had required hemming. She had to drop in on the caterer to go over final arrangements for the reception. She and Varena had to take Anna to a friend's birthday party, and then to pick up Anna's flower girl dress, which was being shipped to the local Penney's catalog store after some delay. (Due to a last-minute growth spurt, Anna's fancy dress, bought months before, was now too tight in the shoulders, so Varena had had to scour catalogs for a quickly purchasable substitute.) Both Varena and my mother were determined that Anna should try the dress on instantly.

The list of errands grew longer and longer. I found myself tuning out after the first few items. Dill dropped Anna off to run errands with Varena and Mom, and Anna and I sat together at the kitchen table in the strange peace that lies at the eye of the storm.

"Is getting married always like this, Aunt Lily?" Anna asked wearily.

"No. You can just elope."

"Elope? Like the animal?"

"It's like an antelope only in that you run fast. When you elope, the man and woman who are getting married get in the car and drive somewhere and get married where nobody knows them. Then they come home and tell their families."

"I think that's what I'm gonna do," Anna told me.

"No. Have a big wedding. Pay them back for all this," I advised.

Anna grinned. "I'll invite everyone in the whole town," she said. "And Little Rock, too!"

"That'll do it." I nodded approvingly.

"Maybe in the whole world."

"Even better."

"Do you have a boyfriend, Aunt Lily?"

"Yes."

"Does he write you notes?" Anna made a squeezed face, like she felt she was asking a stupid question, but she wanted to know the answer anyway.

"He calls me on the phone," I said. "Sometimes."

"Does he . . ." Anna was rummaging in her brain for

other things grown-up boyfriends might do. "Does he send you flowers and candy?"

"He hasn't yet."

"What does he do to show you he likes you?"

Couldn't share that with an eight-year-old. "He hugs me," I told her.

"Ewwww. Does he kiss you?"

"Yeah, sometimes."

"Bobby Mitzer kissed me," Anna said in a whisper.

"No kidding? Did you like it?"

"Ewwww."

"Maybe he's just not the right guy," I said, and we smiled at each other.

Then Mom and Verena told Anna they had been ready to go for minutes and inquired why she was still sitting at the table as if we had all day.

"You can manage at Dill's by yourself, can't you?" Varena asked anxiously. She'd returned from dropping Anna off at the party, complete with present. "You sure don't have to do it if you don't want to."

"I'll be fine," I said, hearing my voice come out flat and cold. I'd enjoyed talking to Anna, but now I felt exhausted again.

Mother eyed me sharply. "You didn't sleep well," she said. "Bad dreams again?" And she and Varena and my father stared at me with matching expressions of concern.

"I'm absolutely all right," I said, trying to be civil, hating them thinking about the ordeal again. Was I being disgustingly self-pitying? It was just being *home*.

For the first time it occurred to me that if I'd been able to stay longer after the attack, if I'd toughed it out, they

156

might have become used to me again, and they would have seen my life as a continuation, not a broken line. But I'd felt compelled to leave, and their clearest, most recent memory of me was of a woman in horrible pain of both kinds, plagued by nightmares waking and sleeping.

"I'll go clean now." I pulled on my coat.

"Dill's at work checking his inventory," Varena said. "I don't know how long he'll be. We'll be picking Anna up and taking her straight to Penney's from the party. Then we'll come back here." I nodded and went to get my purse.

Mother and Varena were still fine-tuning their agenda when I walked out the door. My father was working a crossword puzzle, a half smile on his face as he caught snatches of their discussion. He didn't loathe this wedding frenzy, as most men did or pretended to. He loved it. He was having a great time fussing about the cost of the reception, whether he needed to go to the church to borrow yet another table for the still-incoming gifts, whether Varena had written every single thank-you note promptly.

I touched Father's shoulder as I went by, and he reached up and captured my hand. After a second, he patted it gently and let me go.

Dill owned an undistinguished three-bedroom, three bath ranch-style in the newest section of Bartley. Varena had given me a key. It still felt strange to find a locked door in my little hometown. When I'd been growing up, no one had ever locked anything.

On the way to Dill's, I'd seen another homeless person, this one a white woman. She was gray-haired but sturdy looking, pedaling an ancient bicycle laden down with an assortment of strange items bound together with nylon rope.

The night before, my parents' friends had been talking

about gang activity at the Bartley High School. Gangs! In the Arkansas Delta! In flat, remote, tiny, impoverished Bartley.

I guess in some corner of my mind, I'd expected Bartley would remain untouched by the currents of the world, would retain its small-town safety and assurance. Home had changed. I could go there again, but its character was permanently altered.

Abruptly, I was sick of myself and my problems. It was high time I got back to work.

I started, as I like to do, with a survey of the job to be done. Dill's house, which looked freshly painted and carpeted, was fairly straight and fairly clean—but, like the Osborns', it was showing signs of a few days of neglect. Varena wasn't the only one feeling the effects of prolonged wedding fever.

I had no guide here to show me where everything was. I wondered if Anna would have been as interesting a helper as Eve had been the day before.

That recalled me to the purpose of my cleaning offer. Before anything or anyone could interrupt me, I searched Anna's room for her memory book. As I searched, naturally I picked up her room, which was a real mess. I slung soiled clothes into the hamper, stacked school papers, tossed dolls into a clear Rubbermaid tub firmly labeled "Dolls and doll clothes."

I found the memory book under her bed. Page 23 was missing.

I rocked back on my haunches, feeling as though an adversary had socked me in the stomach.

"No," I said out loud, hearing the misery in my own voice.

After a few minutes trying to think, I stuck the book in the rack on Anna's little desk and kept on cleaning. There was nothing else for me to do.

I had to face the fact that the page that had been sent to Roy Costimiglia and passed to Jack had almost certainly come from Anna's book. But, I told myself, that didn't have to mean Anna was Summer Dawn Macklesby.

The book being in Dill's house perhaps raised the odds that someone besides Meredith Osborn might have mailed the page to Roy Costimiglia. At least, that was what I thought. But I wished I'd found the book anywhere but here.

If Anna was the abducted child, Dill could be suffering from the terrible dichotomy of wanting to square things with Summer's family and wanting to keep his beloved daughter. What if his unstable wife had been the one to kidnap the Macklesby baby, and Dill had just now become aware of it? He'd raised Anna as his own for eight years.

And if Dill's first wife had abducted Summer Dawn, what had happened to their biological baby?

As I paired Anna's shoes and placed them on a rack in the closet, I saw a familiar blue cover peeking from behind a pair of rain boots. I frowned and squatted, reaching back in the closet and finally managing to slide a finger between the book and wall. I fished out the book and flipped it over to read the cover.

It was another copy of the memory book.

I opened it, hoping fervently that Anna had written her name in it. No name.

"Shit," I said out loud. When I'd been young, and we'd gotten our yearbooks, or memory books, or whatever you

159

wanted to call them, the first thing we'd done was write our names inside.

One of these books had to be Anna's. If Jack's basic assumption was correct, if the person who'd sent the memory book page to Roy Costimiglia wasn't a complete lunatic, then the other book belonged to either Eve or Krista, and it was someone very close to one of them who had sent the picture. Like someone in their house. A parent.

Dill was using the third bedroom as a study. There was a framed picture of Dill holding a baby I presumed was Anna. The snapshot had obviously been taken in a hospital room, and Anna looked like a newborn. But to me all babies looked more or less the same, and the infant Dill was gazing at so lovingly could have been Anna, or it could have been another child. The baby was swaddled in a receiving blanket.

I cleaned, scrubbed, and worried at the problem. I straightened and dusted and vacuumed and polished and mopped, and the activity did me good. But I didn't solve anything.

When I went in Anna's room yet again to return a Barbie I'd found in the kitchen, I looked more closely at Anna's collection of framed snapshots. One was of a woman I was sure must be Dill's first wife, Anna's mother. She was buxom, like Varena; and like Varena her hair was brown, her eyes blue. Aside from those superficial similarities, she didn't look at all like my sister, really. I stared at the picture, trying to read the woman's character in this likeness. Was there something tense, something a little desperate, in the way she was clutching the little dog on her lap? Was her smile strained, insincere?

I shook my head. I would never have given the picture two thoughts if I hadn't known that the woman had eventually killed herself. So much despair, so well hidden. Dill had an unstable mother, had married an unstable wife. I was frightened that he could see something deep in Varena that we didn't suspect, some inner weakness, that attracted him or made him feel comfortable with her. But Varena seemed sane and sturdy to me, and I have a built-in Geiger counter for the ripples of instability in others.

It felt odd to see Varena's clothes hanging in half of Dill's closet, her china in his cabinets. She had really and truly moved into Dill's house. That intimacy bore in on me how much Varena would lose if Anna was someone else's daughter, for surely there would be the scandal to end all scandals . . . media coverage, intense and drenching. I shivered. I knew how that could affect your life.

The wedding was so close. One more day.

Very reluctantly, I reentered Dill's office and opened the filing cabinet. I had put on a pair of fresh rubber gloves, and I kept them on. That shows you how guilty I was feeling.

But this *had* to be done.

Dill was an orderly man, and I quickly found the file labeled simply "Anna—Year One." There was a separate file for each year of her life, containing drawings, pictures, and a page of cute things she'd said or done. The school-age files were crammed with report cards and test scores.

As far as I was concerned, Anna's first year was the most important. The file contained Anna's birth certificate, a record of her immunizations, her baby book, and some negatives in a white envelope marked "Baby Is Born." The handwriting wasn't Dill's. There was not a thing there that would prove Anna's identity one way or another. No blood type, no record of any distinguishing characteristic. A certificate from the hospital had Anna's baby footprints in black ink. I would ask Jack if the Macklesbys had similar prints of Summer Dawn's. If the contour of the foot was completely different from Anna's, surely that would mean something?

Blind alley. Dead end.

Suddenly I remember the negatives marked "Birth Pictures." Where were the family photo albums?

I found them in a cabinet in the living room and blessed Dill for being orderly. They were labeled by year.

I yanked out the one marked with Anna's birth year. There were the pictures: a red infant in a doctor's arms, streaked with blood and other fluids, mouth open in a yell; the baby, now held by a masked and gowned Dill, the baby's round little bottom toward the camera—presumably this one had been taken by a nurse. In the corner of the picture, her face just visible, was the woman in the picture in Anna's room. Her mother, Judy.

And on the baby's bottom, a big brown birthmark.

This was proof, wasn't it? This was indisputably a delivery room picture, this was indisputably the baby born to Dill and his wife, Judy. And this baby, shown in a third picture cradled in the arms of the woman in the picture in Anna's room, was absolutely positively the original Anna Kingery.

The elation at finding something certain helped me through the pang of guilt I suffered as I extracted the key picture from the album. It, too, went in my purse, after I'd returned the photo album to its former position.

I finished my cleaning, surveyed the house, found it good. I put the garbage in the wheeled cans, swept the front and back steps. I was done. I went back in to put the broom away.

Dill was standing in the kitchen.

He had a pile of mail in his hands, was shuffling through it. When the broom hit the floor, Dill looked up sharply.

"Hi, Lily, this was mighty fine of you," he said. He smiled at me, his bland and forgettable face beaming nothing but goodwill. "Hey, did I scare you? I thought you heard me pull into the garage."

He must have come in the back door while I was sweeping at the front.

Still tense all over, I bent to retrieve the broom, glad my face was hidden for a moment while I recovered.

"I saw Varena downtown," he said, as I straightened and moved to the broom closet. "I can't believe after all this waiting, it's finally going to be our wedding day tomorrow."

I wrung out a dishrag I'd forgotten and draped it neatly over the sink divider.

"Lily, won't you turn to look at me?"

I turned to meet his eyes.

"Lily, I know you and I have never gotten close. But I don't have a sister, and I hope you'll be one to me."

I was repelled. Emotional appeals were not the way to make a relationship happen.

"You don't know how hard it's always been for Varena."

I raised my eyebrows. "Excuse me?"

"Being your sister."

I took a deep breath. I held my hand palm up. Explain?

"She would kill me if she knew I was saying this." He

shook his head at his own daring. "She never felt as pretty as you, as smart as you."

That didn't matter now. It hadn't mattered for more than a decade.

"Varena," I began, and my voice sounded rusty, "is a grown woman. We haven't been teenagers for years."

"When you're a younger sister, apparently you have baggage you carry with you always. Varena thinks so, anyway. She always felt like an also-ran. With your parents. With your teachers. With your boyfriends."

What crap was this? I gave Dill a cold stare.

"And when you got raped . . ."

I'll give him that, he went right on and said the word.

". . . and all the focus was on you, and all you wanted was to get rid of it, I think in some way it gave Varena some . . . satisfaction."

Which would have made her feel guilty.

"And of course, she began to feel guilty about that, about even feeling a particle of righteousness about your getting hurt."

"Your point being?"

"You don't seem happy to be here. At the wedding. In the town. You don't seem happy for your sister."

I couldn't quite see the connection between the two statements. Was I supposed to wag my tail since Varena was getting married . . . because she'd felt guilty when I got raped? I didn't have any active animosity toward Dill Kingery, so I tried to work through his thought.

I shook my head. I wasn't making any connections. "Since Varena wants to marry you, I'm glad she is," I said cautiously. I wasn't about to apologize for being who I was, what I had become.

164

Dill looked at me. He sighed. "Well, that's as good as it's gonna get, I guess," he said, with a tight little smile.

Guess so.

"What about you?" I asked. "You married one unstable wife. Your mother's not exactly predictable. I hope you see nothing like that in Varena."

He threw back his head and laughed.

"You take the cake, you really do, Lily," he said, shaking his head. He didn't seem to find that endearing. "You don't say much, but you go for the throat when you decide to talk. I think that's what your parents have been dying to ask me for the past two years."

I waited.

"No," he said, quite seriously now. "I see nothing like that in Varena. But that's why I dated her for so long. That's why our engagement went on forever. I had to be sure. For my sake, and especially for Anna's sake. I think Varena is the sanest woman I ever met."

"Did your wife ever threaten to hurt Anna?"

He turned white as a sheet. I'd never seen anyone pale so fast. "What—how—" He was spluttering.

"Before she killed herself, did she threaten to hurt Anna?"

It was like I was a cobra and he was a mouse.

"What have you heard?" he choked out.

"Just a guess. Did she try to hurt Anna?"

"Please go now," he said finally. "Lily, please go."

I'd certainly handled that well. What a masterly interrogation! At least, I reflected, Dill and I had been equally unpleasant to each other, though I might have the edge since I'd talked about something new, something that wasn't common currency in Bartley—at least, judging by Dill's reaction.

I was willing to bet I wouldn't be invited to go on vacations with Dill and Varena.

It seemed possible that Dill's first wife had been capable— at least in Dill's estimation—of harming her baby. And page 23 was missing from a memory book that was most probably Anna's.

I understood what the word "heartsick" meant. I tried to comfort myself with the thought of Anna's birthmark. At least I'd learned one fact.

As I backed out of Dill's driveway I discovered I didn't want to go home.

I began cruising aimlessly—shades of being a teenager, when "riding around" had been a legitimate activity—and didn't know where I was going until I found myself parking at the town square.

I went into the furniture store, and a bell tinkled as the door swung shut. Mary Maude Plummer was typing something into a computer at a desk behind a high counter in the middle of the store. Reading glasses perched at the end of her nose, and she was wearing her business face, competent and no-nonsense.

"Can I help you?" she asked and then looked up from the computer screen. "Oh, Lily!" she said happily, her face changing from the inside out.

"Come go riding," I suggested. "I've got the car."

"Your mom let you have it?" Mary Maude dissolved in giggles. She glanced around at the empty store. "Maybe I can, really! Emory," she called. Out of the shadows at the back of the store, Emory Osborn materialized like a thin, blond ghost.

"Hello, Miss Bard," he said, his voice wispy.

"Emory, can you watch the store while I take my lunch hour?" Mary Maude asked in the gentle, earnest voice you use with slow children. "Jerry and Sam should be back in just a minute."

"Sure," Emory said. He looked as if a good wind would whisk him away.

"Thanks." Mary Maude fished her purse from some hidden spot under the counter.

When we were far enough away that Emory couldn't hear us, Mary Maude muttered, "He should never have tried to come to work today. But his sister's here, and she's managing the home front, so I think he didn't have anything else to do."

We went out the front door like two girls skipping school. I noticed how professional and groomed Mary Maude looked in her winter white suit, a sharp, unwelcome contrast to me in my sweats.

"I've been cleaning Dill's house," I explained, suddenly self-conscious. I couldn't remember apologizing for my clothes, not for years.

"That's what you do for a living now?" Mary Maude asked as she buckled up.

"Yep," I said flatly.

"Boy, did you ever think I'd end up selling furniture and you'd end up cleaning it?"

We shook our heads simultaneously.

"I'll bet you're tops at what you do," Mary said, matter-of-factly.

I was surprised and oddly touched. "I'll bet you sell a lot of furniture," I offered and was even more surprised to find that I meant it.

167

"I do pretty well," she answered, her voice offhand. She looked at me, and her face crinkled in a smile. "You know, Lily, sometimes I just can't believe we grew up!"

That was never my problem. "Sometimes I can't remember I was ever a teen," I said.

"But here we are, alive, in good health, single but not without hope, and backed by family and friends," Mary Maude said, almost chanting.

I raised my eyebrows.

"I have to practice counting my blessings all the time," she explained, and I laughed. "See, that didn't hurt," she said.

We ate lunch at a fast-food place decorated with tinsel and lights and artificial snow. A Santa Claus robot nodded and waved from a plastic sleigh.

For a little while we just got used to each other. We talked about people we'd known and where they were now, how many times they'd been married and to whom. Mary Maude touched on her divorce and the baby she'd lost to crib death. We didn't need to talk about my past; it was too well known. But Mary asked me some questions about Shakespeare, about my daily life, and to my pleasure it was easy to answer.

She, too, asked if I was seeing someone special.

"Yes," I said, trying not to stare down at my hands. "A man from Little Rock. Jack Leeds."

"Oh, is he the ponytail guy who showed up at the wedding rehearsal?"

"Yeah," I said, not even trying to look up this time. "How'd you know?" Why was I even asking, knowing the Bartley grapevine as I did?

"Lou O'Shea was in yesterday. She and Jess have a bed on layaway for Krista for Christmas."

"They seem like a nice couple," I said.

"Yeah, they are," Mary Maude agreed, dipping a french fry in a puddle of ketchup. She'd made a trail of paper napkins to keep her winter white in a pristine state. "They sure are having a hard time with that Krista since they had Luke."

"That's what I hear. You reckon she feels unloved now that the little boy's here?"

"I suppose, though they were real open with her about her being adopted and telling her they loved her enough to pick her out. But I guess maybe she feels like Luke is really theirs, and she isn't."

I said I hadn't realized that the O'Sheas were so open about Krista being adopted.

"Lou more than Jess," Mary Maude commented. "Lou has always been more out-front than her husband, but I guess he's had more practice at keeping secrets, him being a minister and all."

Ministers do have to keep a lot of secrets. I hadn't thought of that before. I got up to get some more tea—and another napkin for Mary Maude.

"Lou tells me the man you're seeing is quite a looker," Mary Maude said slyly, bringing the conversation back to the most interesting topic.

It had never occurred to me someone as conventional as Lou O'Shea would find him so. "Yes."

"Is he sweet to you?" Mary Maude sounded wistful.

This was everyone's day to want to know about Jack. First Anna, now Mary Maude. Weddings must bring it out in women. "Sweet," I said, trying the word on Jack to see how it fit. "No. He's not sweet."

Surprise hiked up Mary Maude's eyebrows. "Not sweet! Well, then! Is he rich?"

169

"No," I answered without hesitation.

"Then why are you seeing him?" Suddenly her cheeks got pinker, and she looked simultaneously delighted and embarrassed. "Is he . . . ?"

"Yes," I told her, trying not to look as self-conscious as I felt.

"Oh, girl," said Mary Maude, shaking her head and giggling.

"Emory is single now," I observed, trying to steer the conversation away from me and into a channel that might lead to some knowledge.

She didn't waste time looking shocked. "Never in a million years," Mary Maude told me as she consumed her last french fry.

"Why are you so sure about that?"

"Aside from the fact that now it would mean taking on a newborn baby and an eight-year-old girl, there's the man himself. I never met anyone as hard to read as Emory. He's polite as the day is long, he never uses bad language, he's . . . yes, he is . . . *sweet*. Old ladies just love him. But Emory's not a simple man, and he's not my idea of red-blooded."

"Oh?"

"Not that I think he's gay," Mary Maude protested hastily. "It's just that, for example, we were outside the store watching the Harvest Festival parade, back in September, and all the beauty queens were coming by riding on the top of the convertibles, like we did?"

I'd completely forgotten that. Maybe that was why riding in the Shakespeare parade had plowed up my feelings so deeply?

"And Emory just wasn't interested. You know? You can

tell when a man is appreciating women. And he wasn't. He enjoyed the floats and the bands. He loved the little girls, you know, Little Miss Pumpkin Patch, that kind of thing, and he told me he'd even thought of entering Eve, but his wife didn't like the idea. But those big gals in their sequin dresses and push-up bras didn't do a thing for Emory. No, I'm going to have to look farther than the furniture store to find someone to date."

I made an indeterminate noise.

"Now, we were talking earlier about Lou and Jess O'Shea. They were watching that parade catty-corner to where I was standing, and believe me, honey! That Jess can enjoy grown-up women!"

"But he doesn't . . . ?"

"Oh, Lord, no! He is devoted to Lou. But he's not blind, either." Mary Maude looked at her watch. "Oh, girl! I have to get back."

We tossed our litter into a can and walked out still talking. Well, Mary Maude was talking, and I was listening, but I was agreeable to listening. And when I dropped her off at Makepeace Furniture, I gave her a quick hug.

I couldn't think of anywhere to go but back to my parents' house.

I walked right into yet another crisis. The couples dinner in honor of Varena and Dill, which had been rescheduled at least twice, was once again endangered. The high school senior who had been booked to baby-sit Krista, her little brother Luke, and Anna had caught the flu.

According to Varena, who was sitting at the kitchen table with the tiny Bartley phone book open before her, she and Lou had called every adolescent known to baby-sit in Bartley, and all of them were either flu victims or already attending a teen Christmas party the Methodist church was giving.

This seemed to be a crisis I had no part in other than to look sympathetic. Then a solution to a couple of problems occurred to me, and I knew what I had to do.

Jack would owe me permanently, as far as I was concerned.

I tapped Varena on the shoulder. "I'll do it," I told her.

"What?" She'd been in the middle of a semihysterical outburst to my mother.

"I'll do it," I repeated.

"You'll . . . baby-sit?"

"That's what I said." I was feeling touchy at the sheer incredulity in my sister's voice.

"Have you *ever* kept kids before?"

"Do you need a baby-sitter or don't you?"

"Yes, it would be wonderful, but . . . are you sure you wouldn't mind? You've never been . . . I mean, you've always said that children weren't your . . . special thing."

"I can do it."

"Well! That would be—just great," Varena said stoutly, obviously realizing she had to show no reservations, no matter what she felt.

Actually, I had kept the four Althaus kids one afternoon and evening when Jay Althaus had been in a car wreck and Carol had had to go to the hospital. Both sets of grandparents had been out of town. Carol had been a frantic, panicked, pathetic mother and wife by the time I answered her phone call.

So I knew how to change diapers and bathe a baby, and

the oldest Althaus boy had showed me how to heat up a bottle. I might not be Mary Poppins, but all the children would be alive and fed and clean by the time the parents got home.

Varena was on the phone with Lou O'Shea, giving her the good news.

"She's glad to do it," Varena was saying, still trying not to sound amazed. "So Lily should be there about, what? Six? Will the kids have eaten? Oh, OK. And there'll be Anna, Krista, your little boy . . . oh, really? Oh, gosh. Let me ask her."

Varena covered the receiver. She was making a big effort to look cheerful and unconcerned. "Lily, Lou says they've agreed to keep the Osborn kids, too. At the time, they thought Shelley was coming with her boyfriend." Shelley was the flu-ridden teenager.

I took a deep, cleansing breath, like I did in karate class before I began my kata. "No problem," I said.

"You're sure?"

I confined myself to a nod.

"That's not a problem, she says," Varena said chirpily into the phone. "Right, it'll only last three hours at the most, two more likely, and we'll be just a few blocks away."

Sounded like Lou was a little concerned at the prospect of my baby-sitting such a mob.

The doorbell rang, and my mother hustled into the living room to answer it. I heard her say, "Hello, again!" with a kind of supercharged enthusiasm that alerted me. Sure enough, she led Jack into the kitchen with a pleased, proud air, as though she'd snagged him just when he was about to get away.

I found myself on my feet and going to him before I

even knew I was moving. His arms slid around me and he gave me a kiss, but a kiss that said my parents were looking at him over my shoulder.

"Well, young man, it's nice to see you again. We'd begun to think we wouldn't get to lay eyes on you before you left town." My father was being bluff and hearty.

Jack was wearing a blue-and-green-plaid flannel shirt and blue jeans, and his thick hair was brushed smoothly back, gathered at the nape of his neck with an elastic band. I patted his shoulder gently and stepped away from him.

"I saw a mighty lot of presents in the living room," Jack said to my father. "Looks like you-all are having a wedding." He smiled, and those seductive deep lines suddenly appeared in parentheses from his nose to the corners of his thin, mobile mouth.

Mother, Father, and Varena laughed, as charmed by his smile as I was.

"As a matter of fact," Jack went on, "I hoped this would be appropriate."

"Why, thank you," Varena said, surprised and showing it, taking the shallow wrapped box Jack pulled out of one jacket pocket.

When I turned to watch Varena opened the present, Jack's arm went around my waist and pulled me against him, my back to his chest. I could feel the corners of my mouth tug up, and I looked down at my hands, resting on the arms crossed below my breasts. I took a deep breath. I made an effort to focus on the box Varena was holding.

She lifted the lid. From the tissue, she extracted an antique silver cake server, a lovely piece with engraving. When Varena passed it around, I could see the curling script read "V K 1889."

"This is just beautiful," Varena said, delighted and not a little stunned. "However did you find it?"

"Sheer luck," Jack said. He was pressed very firmly against my bottom. "I just happened to be in an antiques store and it caught my eye."

I could see the wheels turning in my mother's head. I knew she was thinking that this was a serious present. Such a gift announced that Jack planned to be seeing me for some time, since he was displaying such a great desire to please my family. My father's face lit up (way too obviously) as the same idea occurred to him.

I felt I was watching a tribal ritual unfold.

"I have to put this somewhere conspicuous, so everyone'll notice it," Varena told Jack, plainly wanting him to realize she was very pleased indeed.

"I'm glad you like it," he said.

And before you could say Jack Robinson, Jack Leeds was installed at my parents' kitchen table, a grilled cheese sandwich and bowl of soup in front of him, Varena and my mother waiting on him hand and foot.

After he'd eaten, Mother and Varena practically threw us out of the kitchen so I wouldn't have to help with the dishes. They were flabbergasted when Jack offered to wash. They turned him down with fatuous smiles, and by the time I climbed into Jack's car I was torn between laughter and exasperation.

"I think they approve of me," Jack said with a straight face.

"Well, you *are* breathing."

He laughed, but he stopped abruptly and looked at me with an expression I couldn't decipher. He started the engine.

"Where are we going? I have to be at the manse at 6:00," I reminded him. Mother and Varena had immediately told Jack I'd volunteered to keep the kids.

"We need to talk," he said. We were silent on the ride to the motel, Jack grim and taciturn, I uneasily aware that I was not on the same page.

As we turned on the corner by the Presbyterian manse, I thought of Krista, Anna, and Eve.

And, oddly, I suddenly remembered spending nights with other girls when I was really young. I remembered how I'd carry a whole suitcase full of stuff with me for an overnight visit, everything and anything I thought we might want to play with, or look at, or gossip about.

Including a memory book.

SEVEN

Jack was staying in a different room, since the motel manager was having the bathroom window fixed from the break-in in the room he'd had before.

I was already on edge when we went in, and when Jack sat on one of the stuffed vinyl-covered armchairs, all my systems went on defense. I perched on the edge of the other chair and eyed him warily.

"I saw you last night," he said without preamble.

"Where?"

He sighed. "Out with your old boyfriend."

I made my breathing slow, fighting the rage that swept through me. I gripped the armrests of the damn orange chair. "You got back to town early, and you didn't call me. Did you come back on purpose to spy on me?"

His back stiffened. He was doing a little chair gripping of his own. "Of course not, Lily! I missed you, and I finished what I was doing early, and I drove all afternoon to get back here. Then I saw you in that diner with the cop."

"Were we kissing, Jack?"

"No."

"Were we holding hands, Jack?"

"No."

"Was I looking at him with love, Jack?"

"No."

"Did he look happy, Jack?"

"No." Jack bowed his head, rubbed his forehead with his fingertips.

"Let me tell you what happened the last time I went on a date with Chandler McAdoo, Jack." I bent to his level until he had to look me in the eyes or be a coward. "It was seven years ago, the bad time, and I had been back in Bartley for two months. Chandler and I went to the movies, and then we drove out to the lake, like we'd done when we were kids."

Jack's hazel eyes didn't flinch, and he was listening. I knew it.

"So when we were at the lake, Chandler wanted to kiss me, and I wanted to feel like a real woman again, so I let him. I even enjoyed it . . . a little. And then it went a little farther, and he pulled my T-shirt up. Want to know what happened then, Jack? Chandler started crying. The scars were real fresh then, red. He cried when he saw my body. And that's the last I saw of Chandler for seven years."

A heavy silence settled in the cold motel room.

"Pardon me," Jack said finally. He was absolutely sincere, not mouthing a social catchall. "Pardon me."

"Jack, you never believed I was sneaking behind your back."

"I didn't?" He looked a little angry and a little amused.

"You gave Varena her present before you even discussed last night with me," I said. "You knew all along we weren't . . . parting." I had almost used the phrase "breaking up," but it seemed too childish.

Abruptly, Jack's face went absolutely still, as if he'd had a revelation of some kind.

He turned his eyes to me. "How could he cry?" Jack asked me. "You are so beautiful."

I was still speechless, but for another reason. Jack had never said anything remotely like this.

"Don't pity me," I said softly.

"Lily, you said I never really doubted you. Now, I say, you know that pity is the last thing I feel for you."

He lay with his chest to my back, one arm thrown around me. He was still awake, I could tell. I had another hour and a half, by my watch.

I didn't want to think about Summer Dawn. I didn't want to think about the dead people littering the path to her recovery.

I wanted to touch Jack. I wanted to twine my fingers in his hair. I wanted to understand his thoughts.

But he was a man with a job to do, and he wanted more than anything in the world to take Summer Dawn back to her parents. While he kept his arm around me and from time to time dropped a kiss on my neck, his thoughts had drifted away from me, and mine had to follow.

Reluctantly, I began to tell him what I'd found: the two memory books, one whole and one mutilated, in Anna Kingery's room; the absence of the same book at Eve Osborn's. I told him that Eve Osborn had been to the doctor recently, that I didn't yet know about Anna. I told him about Anna's mother . . . the woman we were assuming was Anna's mother. And I pulled the plastic-wrapped brush and the birth photo of Anna out of my purse and placed them by Jack's briefcase.

I rolled over to face him when I'd finished. I don't know what he saw in my face, but he said, "Damn," under his breath, and looked away from me.

"Have you learned anything?" I asked, to get that expression off his face.

"Like I said, my trip was pretty much of a washout," he told me, but not as if he was upset about it. I guess private eyes encounter a lot of dead-end streets. "But early this morning, I wandered into the police station and took Chandler and a guy named Roger out for coffee and doughnuts. Since I used to be a cop, and they wanted to prove that small-town cops can be just as sharp as city cops, they were pretty forthcoming."

I stroked his hair away from his face and nodded to show him I was listening. I didn't want to tell him they'd have told him nothing if Chandler hadn't checked up on him and talked to me about him.

"They told me the pipe recovered in the alley was definitely the one used to kill the doctor and his nurse," Jack said. "And Christopher Sims's fingerprints were nowhere on it. The pipe has a rusty surface, and some cloth had been run over it. Whoever tried to clean it didn't do a good job. He left one partial. It doesn't match Sims's. He's still in custody for the purse snatching, but I don't think he'll be charged with the murder any time soon."

"Is he making sense?"

"Not a lot. He told the police he'd had a lot of visitors

in his new home, which I gather means the alley behind the stores. That location in the alley is close to every father in this case. Jess O'Shea came to visit Sims as a minister, Emory works in Makepeace Furniture, which backs onto that alley, and Kingery's pharmacy is a block away."

"I noticed that."

"Of course you did," he said and bent to kiss me. My arms went around his neck, and the kiss lasted longer than he thought it was going to. "I want you again," he told me, his voice low and rough.

"I noticed that, too." I pressed against him gently. "But the wedding is tomorrow. Let me tell you about tonight. Since I'm going to baby-sit all the children—Eve, the baby, Krista, Luke, and Anna—at the O'Sheas' house, maybe I can learn something from the children, or from being in that house."

"Where are all the parents going?"

"To a dinner. It's a couples thing, so I was glad to get out of it."

"Who would they have paired you with?" Jack asked.

I realized for the first time that I was causing a hostess some seating problems. "I don't know," I admitted. "I guess that friend of Dill's, Berry Duff."

"Has he been by your folks' much?"

"No, I think he went right home after the rehearsal dinner. He'll come back into town today, if I remember right, and spend the night somewhere here in town. I guess here at the motel."

"He admired you."

"Sure, I'm everyone's dream girl," I said, hearing the sharp edge in my voice, unable to stop it.

"Did you like him?"

What the hell was this? "He's nice enough," I said.

"You could be with him," he said. His light hazel eyes fixed on mine. He didn't blink. "He wouldn't drag you into things like this."

"Hmmm," I said thoughtfully, "Berry is awful cute . . . and he has his own farm. Varena was telling me how beautiful his house is. It's part of the spring garden tour."

For a second Jack's face was a real picture. Then he pounced on me. He pinned me by the shoulders and scooted his body sideways until it lay over mine.

"Are you teasing me, house cleaner?"

"What do you think, detective?"

"I think I've got you where I want you," he said, and his mouth descended.

"Jack," I said after a moment, "I need to tell you something."

"What?"

"Don't ever hold me down."

Jack rolled off instantly, his hands up in a surrender position.

"It's just that you feel so good," he said. "And . . . sometimes I think if I don't weigh you down you'll just drift away." He looked off to the side, then back at me. "What the hell did that mean?" he asked, shaking his head at his own fancy.

I knew exactly what he meant.

"I have to go back to the house," I said. "I'll be at the O'Sheas' from about five-thirty on." I swung myself up and sat with my back to him, since I had to begin getting my clothes out of the heap by the bed.

I felt his hand on my back, stroking. I shivered.

182

"What are you going to do?" I said over my shoulder, as I bent to retrieve my bra.

"Oh, I have an idea or two," he said casually. He hooked the bra for me.

Jack was going to do something illegal.

"Like what?" I pulled my shirt over my head.

"Oh . . . I might get into the doctor's office tonight."

"Who would let you in? You can't possibly be thinking of breaking in?"

"I think it won't be a problem," he assured me.

"You know anything you learn that way isn't real evidence," I said incredulously. "I've watched enough TV to know that."

"Can you think of another way for me to find out their blood types?"

"Blood types? I thought you said Summer Dawn hadn't had her blood typed? And are you sure the blood types would be in a file at Dr. LeMay's office?"

"All three families went to him."

"But how many kids need to have their blood taken?"

"You said Eve had. If I can eliminate at least one of them, that'll be good," he argued. "I realized that there were only a couple of blood types she could be. In fact, it was Chandler's discussion of your high school biology class that reminded me."

"What blood type would Summer Dawn be?"

"Her mother's A and her father's O. So Summer has to be A or O." Jack had been consulting a page from a sheaf of Xeroxed material.

"So if Anna and Eve are type B or AB, they can't be Summer Dawn. It would have to be Krista."

"Right."

"I hope it isn't Anna," I said, sorry immediately I'd said it out loud, and with that edge of desperation in my voice.

"I hope not, too, for your sister's sake," Jack said briskly, and I was even sorrier I'd said anything. I could feel him shoving off my fear, reminding me he had a job to do that he was compelled to finish. I hated the necessity for the reminder. "Here, here's your sock."

"Jack, what if they're all A or O?" I took the sock from him and pulled it on. I had my shoe tied before he answered.

"I don't know. I'll think of something," he said, but not with any hope in his voice. "Maybe that's not the way to go. I'll call Aunt Betty and see if she's got any ideas. I'll be in and out, so try here if you need me. Something's gotta break tonight."

Before I left my folks' house for the O'Sheas', I dialed a Shakespeare number to talk to my friend Carrie Thrush. As I'd hoped, she was still at her office, having seen her last patient just minutes before.

"How are you?"

"Fine," she said, surprise in her voice. "I'll be glad when flu season is over."

"The house is okay?" Carrie had agreed to stop by once or twice, check to make sure the mail carrier had obeyed my "stop mail" card. I hadn't thought it was much of an imposition, since she was dating Claude Friedrich, who lived in the apartment next door. In fact, I would have asked Claude himself to do it if he hadn't been still limping from a leg injury.

"Lily, your house is fine," Carrie said, good-humored toleration in her low voice. "How are you doing?"

"OK," I said grudgingly.

"Well, we'll be glad to see you come home. Oh, you'll want to know this! Old Mr. Winthrop died yesterday, out at his place. He had a massive heart attack at the supper table. Arnita said he just slumped over in the sweet potatoes. She called nine-one-one, but it was too late."

I figured the whole Winthrop family had to be relieved that the old tyrant was dead, but it wouldn't be decent to admit it.

"That family has been through everything this year," Carrie commented, not at all put off by my lack of response.

"I saw Bobo before I left," I told her.

"His Jeep went by your house twice yesterday evening."

"Hmmm."

"He's carrying a big torch."

I cleared my throat. "Well, he'll meet a gal his own age who doesn't kowtow to him because he's a Winthrop. He's just nineteen."

"Right." Carrie sounded amused. "Besides, you have your own private dick." This was Carrie's little term for Jack. She thought it was really funny. She was definitely smiling on the other end of the line. "How is your family?" she asked.

"This wedding has got everyone crazy."

"And speaking of Jack, have you heard from him?"

"He—ahhh—he's here."

"There? In Bartley?" Carry was startled and impressed.

"It's work," I said hastily. "He's got a job here."

"Right. How coincidental!"

"True," I told her warningly. "He's working."

"So you haven't seen him at all, I'm sure."

"Oh, well . . . a couple of times."

"He come by the house?"

"Yes. He did."

"Met your parents," she prompted.

"Well, OK, he did."

"O—kay." She drew out the word as if she'd proved a point. "He coming back to Shakespeare with you?"

"Yes."

"For Christmas?"

"Yes."

"Way to go, Lily!"

"We'll see," I said skeptically. "And you? You'll be there?"

"Yes, I'm cooking and Claude is coming to my house. I was going to go to my folks', even though it's such a long drive, but when I found out Claude was going to be on his own, I told them I'd have to see them in the spring."

"Moving fast, there."

"Nothing to stop us, is there? He's in his forties and I'm in my midthirties."

I said, "No point taking it slow."

"Damn straight!" Carrie's voice grew muffled as she told her nurse to call someone and give him his test results. Then her voice grew clearer. "So you're coming home when?"

"The day after the wedding," I said firmly. "I can't stand it another minute."

She laughed. "See you then, Lily."

"OK. Thanks for checking the house."

"No problem."

We said good-bye and hung up, both with a few things to think about.

I could tell that Carrie's relationship with Chief of Po-

186

lice Claude Friedrich was flourishing. I hoped it would last. I'd liked both of them for months before they'd ever looked at each other.

I found myself wondering how Bobo was feeling about the death of his grandfather. I was sure he felt some grief, but it must be at least a little mixed with relief. Now Bobo and his parents would have some peace, some time to recoup. It was almost possible they would rehire me.

I dragged myself back to the here and now. It was nearly time for me to go to my baby-sitting stint. I would be in the O'Sheas' house; I could search it as I had the Kingery house and the Osborn house. I was staring at myself in the mirror in the bathroom, refluffing my hair and powdering my face, when I finally registered how miserable I looked.

Couldn't be helped.

In my room, I pulled on my Christmas sweatsuit, the one I'd worn in the parade. I guess I thought the bright color might make me seem more kid-friendly. I ate a bowl of left-over fruit salad, all that I could find in the refrigerator since everyone else in the house was going to the supper.

Dill's friend Berry Duff rang the doorbell while I was washing up, and I let him in. He smiled down at me.

"You look cheerful," he remarked.

"I'm going to baby-sit."

His face fell. "Oh, I was looking forward to talking to you at the dinner."

"Last-minute emergency. The baby-sitter came down with the flu and they couldn't find another one."

"I hope it goes smoothly," Berry said, rather doubtfully, I thought. "I have kids of my own, and a handful at a time is kind of a rough evening."

"How old are yours?" I asked politely.

"I got one who's nine, one who's in the tenth grade . . . let's see . . . Daniel's fifteen now. They're both good kids. I don't get to see them often enough."

I remembered that his wife had custody of the children. "Do they live close enough for you to see them regularly?" I asked.

"Every other weekend," he answered. He looked sad and angry. "That's just not as good, nowhere near as good, as watching them grow up every day." He folded himself into one of the kitchen chairs, and I returned to the sink to finish drying the dishes.

"But you know where they are," I said, surprising even myself. "You know that they're safe. You can pick up the phone and call them."

Berry stared at me in understandable surprise. "That's true," he said slowly, feeling his way. "I'm sure the situation could be worse. You're saying, if my wife ran off with them, went underground, like some spouses do to keep the other parent away from the kids? That would be horrible. I guess I'd just go crazy." Berry mulled it over for a minute. "I'd do anything to get them back, if that happened," he concluded. He looked up at me. "My God, girl, how did we get on this depressing topic? This is supposed to be a happy household! Wedding tomorrow!"

"Yes," I said. "Wedding tomorrow." I had to be resolute. This was not a problem I could solve by hitting or kicking. I puzzled Berry further by patting his shoulder, before I pulled on my coat and called good-bye to my parents.

I thought there was something I'd forgotten to tell Jack today, something small but important. But I couldn't make it float to the surface of my mind.

. . .

The O'Sheas had plenty of room in the Presbyterian manse, since the preacher for whom the home had been built had been the father of five. Of course, that had been in 1938. Now the manse was an underinsulated money pit in need of complete rewiring, Lou told me within the first five minutes after my arrival. I could see that she had some legitimate gripes, because the long, narrow shape of the living area made it hard to group furniture, just for starters. And though there was a fireplace, and it was decorated for the season, the chimney needed so much repair that it wasn't functional.

The preacher's wife was encased in a sage green suit and black suede pumps. Her dark hair was carefully turned under all the way around in a smooth pageboy, and her ski-jump nose had been minimized by some subtle makeup. Lou was clearly looking forward to getting out of her house without the kids in tow, but just as clearly she was little anxious about my keeping them. She was doing her best not to show her worry, but the third time she pointed out the list of emergency phone numbers right by the telephone, I had a very sharp answer practically tottering on the edge of my tongue.

Instead, of course, I took a cleansing breath and nodded. But there may have been something grim in the set of my mouth, because Lou did a double take and apologized profusely for being overprotective. To cut short her apologies, she bent to plug in the Christmas tree, which almost filled a quarter of the room.

The lights began to blink.

I clenched my teeth to keep from saying something Lou was sure to find unacceptable.

The manse seemed as commercial as any other house tricked out for the season, with long plastic candy canes propped on either side of the nonfunctional hearth, where fireplace tools would ordinarily stand. A silver garland was draped between the corners of the mantelpiece, and Lou had hung long plastic icicles from the garland.

Opposite the hearth was a central window before which the tree was positioned. However, under the tree, instead of presents there stood a nativity scene, with a wooden stable and a full complement of shepherds, Joseph and Mary, camels and cows, and the baby Jesus in a manger.

Handsome Jess strode into the room, wearing a dark suit enlivened by a fancy Christmas vest. He was carrying Meredith Osborn's baby, Jane, and Jane was not happy.

It was time for me to prove my worth. I steeled myself to hold out my arms, and he placed the shrieking Jane in them.

"Is she due for a bottle?" I yelled.

"No," bellowed Jess, "I just fed her."

Then she needed burping. After eating came burping, then excreting, then sleeping. This was what I had learned about babies. I turned Jane so she was upright and pointed over my shoulder and began patting her gently with my right hand. Little red-faced thing . . . she was so tiny. Jane had wisps of curling blond hair here and there on her smooth head. Her eyes were squeezed shut with rage, but as soon as I turned her upright she seemed to be crying with less volume. Her little eyes opened and looked hazily at me.

"Hi," I said, feeling I should talk to her.

The other children came piling into the room. Krista's little brother Luke was a cement block of a toddler, so square and heavy that he stomped rather than walked. He was dark-haired like Lou, but he would have the heavy-jawed good looks of his father.

The most amazing belch erupted from the baby. Her body relaxed against my shoulder, which suddenly felt wet.

"Oh, dear," Lou said. "Oh, Lily . . ."

"Should have slung a diaper over your shoulder." Jess's advice was just a little too late.

I looked directly into the baby's eyes, and she made one of those little baby noises. Her tiny hands flailed the air.

"I'll hold her while you clean up," Eve volunteered, while Krista said, "Ewww! Look at the white stuff on Miss Lily's shoulder!"

"Sit in the chair," I told Eve.

Eve settled herself in the nearest armchair, her legs crossed on the seat. I settled Eve's sister into her lap and checked to make sure that Eve was holding the baby correctly. She was.

Followed by the herd of kids, I went to the bathroom, got a washcloth out of the linen closet, and dampened it to rub the worst of the belched liquid off my shoulder. I didn't want to smell it all night. Krista kept up a running commentary the whole time, Anna seemed conflicted between being sympathetic toward her future aunt and rolling in the grossness of baby throw up like Krista, and Luke just stared while holding his left ear with his left hand and gripping the hair on the top of his head with his right, a posture that made him look like he was receiving signals from another planet.

I realized that Luke was probably still wearing diapers, too.

The O'Sheas called good-bye as they escaped from the

houseful of children, and I tossed the washrag into the dirty clothes hamper and glanced at my watch. It was time to change Jane.

I settled Luke in the far end of the living room in front of the television, watching a Christmas cartoon and communicating with Mars. He chose to sit almost inside the branches of the Christmas tree. The blinking didn't seem to bother him.

The girls all followed me to the baby's room. Eve was proprietary because the baby was her sister, Krista was hoping to see poop so she could provide running commentary on its grossness, and Anna was still waiting to see which way the wind blew.

Grabbing a fresh disposable diaper, I placed the baby on the changing table and went through the laborious and complicated process of unsnapping the crotch of Jane's sleeper. Mentally reviewing how I'd changed the Althaus baby, I opened the pull tabs on the old diaper, lifted Jane by the legs, removed the soiled diaper, pulled a wipe from the box on the end of the changing table, cleaned the pertinent areas, and pushed the new diaper under Jane. I ran the front part between her tiny legs, pulled the adhesive tabs shut, and reinserted the baby into the sleeper, getting the snaps wrong only one time.

The three girls decided this was boring. I watched them troop through the door to go to Krista's room. They were so superficially similar, yet so different. All were eight years old, give or take a few months; all were within three inches of being the same height; they had brown hair and brown eyes. But Eve's hair was long and looked as if someone had taken a curling iron to it, and Eve was thin and pale. Krista, blocky and with higher color, had short, thick, darker hair and a more decisive demeanor. Her jaw jutted out like she was about to take it on the chin. Anna had shoulder-length light brown hair, a medium build, and a ready smile.

One of these three little girls was not who she thought she was. Her parents were not the people she had always identified as her parents. Her home was not really her home; she belonged elsewhere. She was not the oldest child in the family but the youngest. Everything in her life had been a lie.

I wondered what Jack was doing. I hoped whatever it was, he wouldn't get caught.

I carried the baby into the living room with me. Luke was still absorbed in the television, but he half turned as I entered and asked me for a snack.

With the attention to detail you have to have around kids, I put Jane in her infant seat, fastened the strap and buckle arrangement that prevented her from falling out, and fetched Luke a banana from the chaotic kitchen.

"I want chips. I don't like nanas," he said.

I exhaled gently. "If you eat your banana, I'll get you some chips," I said as diplomatically as I am able. "After supper. I'll be putting supper on the table in just a minute."

"Miss Lily!" shrieked Eve. "Come look at us!"

Ignoring Luke's continued complaints about bananas, I strode down the hall to the room that must be Krista's, judging from all the signs on the door warning Luke never to come in.

It didn't seem possible the girls could have done so much to themselves in such a short time. Both Krista and Anna were daubed with makeup and swathed in full dress-up regalia: net skirts, feathered hats, tiny high heels. Eve, sitting on Krista's bed, was much more modestly decked out, and she wore no makeup at all.

I looked at Krista's and Anna's lurid faces and had a flash of horror before I realized that if all this stuff had been in Krista's room, this must be an approved activity.

"You look . . . charming," I said, having no idea what an acceptable response would be.

"I'm the prettiest!" Krista said insistently.

If the basis for selection was heavy makeup, Krista was right.

"Why don't you wear makeup, Miss Lily?" Eve asked.

The three girls crowded around and analyzed my face.

"She's got mascara on," Anna decided.

"Red stuff? Rouge?" Krista was peering at my cheeks.

"Eye shadow," Eve said triumphantly.

"More isn't always better," I said, to deaf ears.

"If you wore a lot of makeup, you'd be beautiful, Aunt Lily," Anna said surprisingly.

"Thank you, Anna. I'd better go see how the baby is."

Luke had unsnapped the baby's sleeper and pulled it from her tiny feet. He was bending over her with a pair of tiny, sharp fingernail scissors.

"What are you doing, Luke?" I asked when I could draw my breath.

"I'm gonna help you out," he said happily. "I'm gonna cut baby Jane's toenails."

I shuddered. "I appreciate your wanting to help. But you have to wait for Jane's daddy to say whether or not he wants you to do that." That seemed pretty diplomatic to me.

Luke insisted vehemently that Jane's long toenails were endangering her life and had to be trimmed now.

I began to dislike this child very seriously.

"Listen to me," I said quietly, cutting right through all his justification.

194

Luke shut right up. He looked plenty scared.

Good.

"Don't touch the baby unless I ask you to," I said. I thought I was making a simple declarative sentence, but possibly Luke was good at interpreting voice tone. He dropped the scissors. I picked them up and shoved them in my sweatpants pocket where I could be certain he wouldn't reclaim them.

I picked up the infant seat and took Jane into the kitchen with me to set out the children's meal. Lou had left canned funny-shaped pasta in sauce, which I wouldn't have fed to my dog, if I'd had one. I heated it, trying not to inhale. I spooned it into bowls, then cut squares of Jell-O and put them on plates, adding apple slices that Lou had already prepared. I poured milk.

The kids ran in and scooted into chairs the minute I called them, even Luke. Without prompting, they all bowed their heads and said the "God is great" prayer in unison. I was caught flat-footed, halfway to the refrigerator to put the milk carton away.

The next fifty minutes were . . . trying.

I understand that close to Christmas children get excited. I realize that children in packs are more excitable than children separately. I have heard that having a sitter instead of parental supervision causes kids to push their limits, or rather, their sitter's. But I had to take several deep breaths as the kids rampaged through their supper. I perched on a stool, baby Jane in her infant seat on the kitchen counter beside me. Jane, at least, was asleep. A sleeping baby is a near-perfect thing.

As I wiped up slopped tomato sauce, put more sliced apples into Luke's bowl, stopped Krista from poking Anna with a spoon, I gradually became aware that Eve was quieter than the others. She had to make a visible effort to join in the hilarity.

Of course, her mother had just died.

So I kept a wary eye on Eve.

Far from planning to learn something that evening, I was beginning to hope merely to survive it. I'd thought I'd get a moment to look for family records. That was so clearly impossible, I was convinced I'd leave as ignorant as when I'd come.

Krista took care of the problem for me.

Reaching for the crackers I'd set in the center of the table, she knocked over her milk, which cascaded off the table into Anna's lap. Anna shrieked, called Krista a butthead, and darted a terrified glance at me. This was not approved language in the Kingery household, and since I was almost her aunt, I gave Anna the obligatory stern look.

"Do you have a change of pants here?" I asked.

"Yes ma'am," said a subdued Anna.

"Krista, you wipe up the milk with this towel while I take Anna to change. I'll need to put those pants right in the washer."

I picked up the baby in her infant seat and carried her with me down the hall, trying not to jostle her from her sleep. Anna hurried ahead of me, wanting to change and get back to her friends.

I could tell that Anna was not comfortable taking off her clothes with me in the room, but we'd done a little bonding that morning and she didn't want to hurt my feelings by asking me to leave. God knows I hated invading anyone's privacy, but I had to do it. After I found a safe spot on the floor for Jane, I picked up the room while Anna untied her shoes and divested herself of her socks, pants, and panties. I had my back to her, but I was facing a mirror when her panties came down, and since she had her back to me, I was able to see clearly the dark brown splotch of the birthmark on her hip.

I had to lean against the wall. A wave of relief almost bowled me over. Anna having that birthmark simply had to mean that Anna was the baby in the birth picture with her mother and Dill, their original and true child, and not Summer Dawn Macklesby.

I had something to be thankful for, after all.

I picked up the wet clothes, and Anna, having pulled on some dry ones, dashed out of the room to finish her supper.

I was about to pick up Jane when Eve came in. She stood, her arms behind her back, looking at her shoes. Something about the way she was standing put me on full alert.

"Miss Lily, you remember that day you came to our house and cleaned up?" she asked, as though it had been weeks before.

I stood stock still. I saw myself opening the box on the shelf. . . .

"Wait," I told her. "I want to talk to you. Wait just one moment."

The nearest telephone, and the one that was the most private, was the one in the master bedroom across the hall.

I looked through the phone book, found the number of Jack's motel. Please let him be there, please let him be there . . .

Mr. Patel connected me to Jack's room. Jack answered on the second ring.

"Jack, open your briefcase," I said.

Some assorted sounds over the other end.

197

"OK, it's done."

"The picture of the baby."

"Summer Dawn? The one that was in the paper?"

"Yes, that one. What is the baby wearing?"

"One of those one-piece things."

"Jack, what does it look like?"

"Ah, long arms and legs, snaps . . ."

"What is the *pattern?*"

"Oh. Little animals, looks like."

I took a deep, deep breath. "Jack, what kind of animal?"

"Giraffes," he said, after a long, analytical pause.

"Oh God," I said, scarcely conscious of what I was saying.

Eve came into the bedroom. She had picked up the baby and brought her with her. I looked at her white face, and I am sure I looked as stricken as I felt.

"Miss Lily," she said, and her voice was limp and a little sad. "My dad's at the door. He came to get us."

"He's here," I said into the phone and hung up.

I got on my knees in front of Eve. "What were you going to tell me?" I asked. "I was wrong to go use the phone when you were waiting to talk to me. Tell me now."

My intensity was making her nervous, I could see, but it wasn't something I could turn off. At least she knew I was taking her seriously.

"He's here now, it's . . . I have to go home."

"No, you need to tell me." I said it as gently as I could, but firmly.

"You're strong," she said slowly. Her eyes couldn't meet mine. "My dad said my mom was weak. But you're not."

"I'm strong." I said it flatly, with as much assurance as I could pack into a statement.

"Maybe . . . you could tell him me and Jane need to spend the night here, like we were supposed to? So he won't take us home?"

She'd intended to tell me something else.

I wondered how much time I had before Emory came to find out what was keeping us.

"Why don't you want to go home?" I asked, as if we had all the time in the world.

"Maybe if he really wanted me to come, Jane could stay here with you?" Eve asked, and suddenly tears were trembling in her eyes. "She's so little."

"He won't get her."

Eve looked almost giddy with relief.

"You don't want to go," I said.

"Please, no," she whispered.

"Then he won't get you."

Telling a father he couldn't have his kids was not going to go over well. I hoped Jack had found something, or Emory would make that one wrong move.

He'd have to. He'd have to be provoked.

Time to take my gloves off.

"Stay here," I told Eve. "This may get kind of awful, but I'm not letting anyone take you and Jane out of this house."

Eve suddenly looked frightened by what she had unleashed, realizing on some level that the monster was out of the closet now, and nothing would make it go back in. She had taken her life, and her sister's, in her own hands at the ripe old age of eight. I am sure she was wishing she could take back her words, her appeal.

"It's out of your hands now," I said. "This is grown-up stuff."

She looked relieved, and then she did something that sent shivers down my back: She picked up the baby in her carrier and took her to a corner of the bedroom, pulling out the straight-backed chair that blocked it, crouching down behind it with the baby beside her.

"Throw Reverend O'Shea's bathrobe over the chair," the little voice suggested. "He won't find us, maybe."

I felt my whole body clench. I picked up the blue velour bathrobe that Jess had left lying across the foot of the bed and draped it over the chair.

"I'll be back in a minute," I said and went down the hall to the living room, Anna's milk-stained clothes still under my arm. I tossed them into the washroom as I passed it. I was trying to keep things as normal as I could. There were children here, in my care.

Emory was standing just inside the front door. He was wearing jeans and a short jacket. He'd pulled his gloves off and stuck them in a pocket. His blond hair was brushed smooth, and he looked as if he'd just shaved. It was like . . . I hesitated to say this, even to myself.

It was like he was here to pick up his date.

His guileless blue eyes met mine with no hesitation. Luke, Anna, and Krista were playing a video game at the other end of the room.

"Hey, Miss Bard." He looked a little puzzled. "I sent Eve back to tell you I'd decided the girls should spend the night at home, after all. I've imposed on the O'Sheas too much."

I walked over to the television. I had to turn off the screen before the children would look at me. Krista and Luke were surprised and angry, though they were too well

200

raised to say anything. But Anna somehow knew that something was wrong. She stared at me, her eyes as round as quarters, but she didn't ask any questions.

"You three go back and play in Krista's room," I said. Luke opened his mouth to protest, took a second look at me, and jumped up to run back to his sister's room. Krista gave me a mutinous glare, but when Anna, casting several backward looks, followed Luke, Krista left too.

Emory had moved closer to the hall leading down to the bedrooms. He was leaning on the mantel, in fact. He'd pulled off his jacket. He was still smiling gently at the children as they passed him. I moved closer.

"The girls are going to stay here tonight," I said.

His smile began to twitch around the edges. "I can take my children when I want, Miss Bard," he told me. "I'd thought I needed time alone with my sister to plan the funeral service, but she had to go home to Little Rock tonight, so I want my girls to come home."

"The girls are going to stay here tonight."

"Eve!" he bellowed suddenly. "Come out here right now!"

I heard the children in Krista's room fall silent.

"Stay where you are!" I called, hoping each and every one of them understood I meant it.

"How can you tell me I can't have my kids?" Emory looked almost tearful, not angry, but there was something in the way he was standing that kept me on the edge of wary.

Truth or dare. "I can tell you that so easy, Emory," I said. "I know about you."

Something scary flared in his expression for just a second. "What the heck are you talking about?" he said, permitting himself to show a reasonable anger and disgust. "I came to get my little girls! You can't keep my little girls if I want them!"

"Depends on what you want them for, you son of a bitch."

It was the bad language that cracked Emory's facade.

He came at me then. He grabbed one of the plastic icicles suspended from the garland on the O'Sheas' mantel, and if I hadn't caught his wrist, it would have been embedded in my neck. I overbalanced while I was keeping the tip away from my throat, and over we went. As Emory and I hit the floor with a thud, I could hear the children begin to wail, but it seemed far away and unimportant just now. I'd fallen sideways, and my right hand was trapped.

Emory was small and looked frail, but he was stronger than I'd expected. I was gripping his forearm with my left hand, keeping the hard plastic away from my neck, knowing that if he succeeded in driving it in I would surely die. His other hand fastened around my neck, and I heard my own choking noises.

I wrenched my shoulder in a desperate effort to pull my right hand out from under my body. Finally it was free, and I found my pocket. I pulled out the nail scissors and sunk them into Emory's side.

He howled and yanked sideways, and somehow I lost the scissors. But now I had two free hands. With both of them I forced his right hand back, heaved myself against him, and over we rolled with me on top but with his left hand still digging into my throat. I pushed his right arm back and down, though his braced left arm kept me too far away to force it to the ground and break it. I struggled to straddle him and finally managed it. By now I was seeing a wash of gray strewn with spots instead of living room furniture. I pushed up on my knees and then let my weight fall down on him as hard as I could. The air whooshed out of Emory's lungs then, and he was trying to gasp for oxygen, but I thought maybe I would give out first. I raised up and collapsed on him again, but like a snake he took advantage of my movement to start to roll on his side, and since I was pushing his right arm in that direction, I went, too, and now we were on the floor under the Christmas tree, the tiny colored lights blinking, blinking.

I could see the lights blinking through the gray fog, and they maddened me.

Abruptly, I let go of Emory's arm and snatched a loop of lights from the tree branches. I swung the loop around Emory's neck, but I wasn't able to switch hands to give myself a good cross pull. He drove the tip of the plastic icicle into my throat.

The plastic tip was duller than a knife, and I am muscular, so it still hadn't penetrated by the time the string of blinking lights around Emory's neck began to take effect.

He took his left hand from my throat to claw at the lights, his major error since I'd been right on the verge of checking out of consciousness. I was able to roll my head to the side to minimize the pressure of the icicle. I was doing much better until Emory, scrabbling around with that left hand, seized the stable of the manger scene and brought it down on my head.

I was out only a minute, but in that minute the room had emptied and the house had grown silent. I rolled to my knees and pushed up on the couch. I took an experimental step. Well, I could walk. I didn't know how much more I was capable of doing, but I seized the nearest thing I could strike with, one of the long plastic candy canes that Lou had set on each side of the hearth, and I started down the hall, pressing myself against the wall. I passed the washroom on my left and a closet on my right. The next door on my left was Krista's room. The door was open.

I cautiously looked around the door frame. The three children were sitting on Krista's bed, Anna and Krista with their arms around each other, Luke frantically sucking on his fingers and pulling his hair. Krista gave a little shriek when she saw me. I put my finger across my lips, and she nodded in a panicky way. But Anna's eyes were wide and staring as if she was trying to think of how to tell me something.

I wondered if they would trust me, the mean stranger they didn't know, or Emory, the sweet man they'd seen around for years.

"Did he find Eve?" I asked, in a voice just above a whisper.

"No, he didn't," Emory said and stepped out from behind the door. He'd gone by the kitchen; I saw by the knife in his hand.

Anna screamed. I didn't blame her.

"Anna," said Emory. "Sweet little girls don't make noise." Anna choked back another scream, scared to death he would get near her, and the resulting sound was terrifying. Emory glanced her way.

I stepped all the way into the room, raised the plastic candy cane, and brought it down on Emory's arm with all the fury I had in me.

"*I'm* not sweet," I said.

He howled and dropped the knife. I put one foot on it

and scooted it behind me with the toe of my shoe, just as Emory charged. The plastic candy cane must not have been very intimidating.

This time I was ready, and as he lunged toward me, I stepped to one side, stuck out one foot, and as he stumbled over it, I brought the candy cane down again on the back of his neck.

If the children hadn't been there I would have kicked him or broken one of his arms, to make sure I wouldn't have to deal with him again. But the children were there, Luke screaming and wailing with all the abandon of a two-year-old, and Anna and Krista both sobbing.

Would hitting him again be any more traumatic for them? I thought not and raised my foot.

But Chandler McAdoo said, "No."

All the fight went out of me in a gust. I let the red-and-white-striped plastic fall from my fingers to the carpet, told myself I should comfort the children. But I realized in a dim way that I was not at all comforting right now.

"Eve and Jane are behind the chair in the bedroom across the hall," I said. I sounded exhausted, even to myself.

"I know," Chandler said. "Eve called nine-one-one."

"Miss Lily?" called a tiny, shaky voice.

I made myself plod into the master bedroom. Eve's head popped up from behind the chair. I sat on the end of the bed.

"You can bring Jane out now," I said. "Thank you for calling the police. That was so smart, so brave." Eve pushed the chair out and picked up the infant seat, though now it was almost too heavy for her thin arms.

Chandler shut the door.

It promptly came open again and Jack came in.

He paused and looked me over. "Anything broken?" he asked.

"No." I shook my head and wondered for a second if I would be able to stop. It felt like pendulum set in motion. I rubbed my throat absently.

"Bruise," said Jack. I watched him try to decide how to approach me and Eve.

With great effort, I lifted my hand and patted Eve on the head. Then I folded her in my arms as she began to cry.

I sat with Eve in my lap that night as she told the police what had been happening in the yellow house on Fulbright Street. Chandler was there, and Jack—and Lou O'Shea, since Jess had passionately wanted to be there as Eve's pastor, but Eve had shown a definite preference for Lou.

Daddy, it seemed, had started getting funny when it became apparent that the bills from Meredith's pregnancy and delivery were going to be substantial. He began to enjoy playing with his eight-year-old daughter.

"He always liked me to wear lipstick and makeup," Eve said. "He liked me to play dress up all the time."

"What did your mom have to say about that, Eve?" Chandler asked in a neutral voice.

"She thought it was funny, at first."

"When did things change?"

"About Thanksgiving, I guess."

It was just after Thanksgiving that the article about unsolved crimes had appeared in the Little Rock paper. With the picture of the baby in the giraffe sleeper. The same baby sleeper that Meredith had kept all these years in a box on the closet shelf, as a memento of her baby's first days.

"Mama wasn't happy. She'd walk around the house and

cry. She had a hard time taking care of Jane. She . . ." Eve's voice dropped almost to a whisper. "She asked me funny questions."

"About . . . ?" Chandler again.

"About did Daddy touch me funny."

"Oh. What did you tell her?" Chandler sounded quiet and respectful of Eve, as if this was a very ordinary conversation. I had not known my old friend could be this way.

"No, he never touched me . . . there. But he liked to play Come Here Little Girl."

My stomach heaved.

I won't go through it all, but the gist of it was that Emory liked to deck Eve in lipstick and rouge and call her over to him as if they were strangers and induce her to touch him through his pants.

"So what else happened?" Chandler asked after a moment.

"He and Mama had a fight. Mama said they had to talk about when I was born, and Daddy said he wouldn't, and Mama said . . . oh, I don't remember."

Had Meredith asked him if Eve was their baby? Had she asked him if he was molesting the child?

"Then Mama or Daddy got my memory book and took a page out of it. I didn't see them do it, but when I got home one day, the page was missing, my favorite picture of me and Anna and Krista. It had been cut out real neat, so I think Mama did it. So the next time I spent the night with Anna, I took it over there with me, so Mama couldn't cut out any more pages."

Jack and I met each other's eyes.

"Then Mama said I needed a blood test. So I went to Dr. LeMay, and he and Miss Binnie took some blood and said they were going to test it, and I had sure been a good girl, and he gave me a piece of candy.

"Mama told me not to tell anyone, but Daddy saw the needle mark when he bathed me that night! But I didn't tell, I didn't!" Big tears rolled down Eve's cheeks.

"No one thinks you did anything wrong," I said.

I hadn't realized how tense she was until she relaxed.

"So Daddy found out. I think he went looking and found the paper Mama got from the doctor."

The lab results? A receipt for whatever Meredith had paid for the blood test?

"So the next night he said Mama needed a break and he was going to take us out."

"And you got in the car, right?" Chandler asked.

"Yep, me and Jane. I was buckling her car seat when Daddy said he'd left his gloves. He opened the trunk and got something out and put it on, and he went in the house. After a few minutes he came back out with something under his arm, and he put it in the trunk and we went out to eat. When we got home . . ." Eve began to cry in earnest then.

Chandler slipped out with Emory's keys to open Emory's trunk. He came back in five minutes.

"I got some people looking and taking pictures," he said quietly. "Come on, sweetie, let's put you on a bed for a little while, so you can lie still."

Lou, who had tears running down her face, held out her arms to Eve, and Eve allowed Lou to pick her up and carry her off.

"What was in the trunk?" Jack asked.

"A clear plastic raincoat with lots of stains and a single-edge kitchen knife."

I shuddered.

Jack and Chandler began to have a very important talk.

Chandler called over to the men searching the house on Fulbright Street. In about thirty minutes, thin Detective Brainerd brought a familiar shoe box into the bedroom at the manse.

Jack put on gloves, opened the box, and began to smile.

Dill and Varena had taken Anna home long before, and I could assume they'd made a report to my parents about where I was.

Jack dropped me at his motel room while he went to the jail to have a conversation with Emory Osborn.

When he returned, I was still lying on the bed staring at the ceiling. I still had my coat on. My throat hurt.

Without speaking, Jack consulted an address book he fished out of his briefcase. Then he picked up the phone, took a deep breath, and began dialing.

"Roy? How you doing? Yeah, I know what time it is. But I thought you should be the one to call Teresa and Simon. Tell them we got the little girl . . . of course I wouldn't kid about something like that. No, I don't want to call them, it's your case." Jack held the phone away from his ear, and I could hear Roy Costimiglia shouting on the other end. When the sound had abated a little, Jack started talking, telling Roy as much as he could in a few sentences.

"No, I don't know . . . they better call their lawyer, have her come down before they come down. I think there's a lot of steps to go through, but Osborn actually admitted it. Yeah." Jack eased back on the bed until he was lying beside me, his body snug against mine. "He delivered his own baby at home, and the baby died. I think there's something kinda hinky about that, it was a baby boy . . . and he definitely likes little girls. Anyway, he felt guilty and he couldn't tell his wife. He gave her a strong painkiller he'd been taking for a back injury, she conked out, he began riding around trying to think of how to tell her the baby didn't make it. He lived right close to Conway, and he found himself just cruising through Conway at random, he says. Yeah, I don't know whether to buy that, either, especially in view . . . wait, let me finish." Jack pulled off his shoes. "He says he rode through the Macklesbys' neighborhood, recognized the house because he'd delivered a couch there about four months before. He liked Teresa, thought she was pretty. Suddenly he remembered that Teresa had been pregnant, wondered if she'd had the baby . . . he watched the house for a while, says he was too distraught to go home and face his wife. Suddenly, he got his chance to make everything better. He saw Teresa come out onto the porch with the baby in her carrier, stop, put her down, and go back in the house. She was such a bad mother she didn't deserve a baby, he decided, and she already had two, anyway. His wife didn't have one. He took Summer Dawn home with him."

Roy must have been talking again. I could feel my eyes grow heavy now that Jack's warmth relaxed me. I turned on my side facing him, my eyes closing just for a minute since he had the bedside lamp on and the glare was unpleasant.

"He took Meredith to the doctor the next day, told the doctor that he'd taken the baby to a pediatrician already. He couldn't have their doctor examine the baby, because he figured that the umbilical thingy was more healed than it would be on a one-day-old baby."

Roy talked for a minute. It was a distant buzz. I kept my eyes shut.

"Yeah, he's confessed all the way. Says it was all his wife's fault for having a baby that died and it being a boy, for interrupting his fun with the little girl he'd so thoughtfully gotten for her, for beginning to wonder where that little girl had come from when she saw the photo in the paper . . . evidently, Meredith took the little girl in for a blood test, found out she couldn't be her daughter. But she loved her so much, she couldn't make up her mind what to do. Emory found out about the blood test, decided Meredith was a traitor, and killed her. He broke into my hotel room, found the pages she'd mailed me . . . it made him feel justified."

Some more talk.

Then Jack asked, "You gonna call them now or wait till the morning?"

Sometime after that, I lost track of what Jack was saying.

"Baby?"

I blinked. "What?"

"Baby, it's morning."

"What?"

"You got to go home and get ready for the wedding, Lily."

My eyes flew open. It was definitely daytime. In a panic, I glanced at the bedside clock. I exhaled a long sigh of relief when I saw it was only eight o'clock.

Jack was standing by the bed. He'd just gotten out of the shower.

Normally in the morning I jump out of bed and get moving, but I felt so groggy. Then I remembered the night before, and I knew where I was.

"Oh, I do have to get home, I hope they're not worried," I said. "I've been so good this whole visit, I've done everything right! I hate to blow it the last day."

Jack laughed. It was a good sound.

I sat up. He'd taken my coat off some time during the night. I'd slept in my clothes, with no shower, and I needed to brush my teeth in the worst possible way. When Jack bent down to hug me, I backed off.

"No no no," I said firmly. "Not now. I'm disgusting."

When Jack saw I meant it, he perched in one of the vinyl chairs. "Want me to go get us some coffee?" he asked.

"Oh, bless you for thinking of it, but I better get to my folks' and let them see me."

"Then I'll see you at the wedding."

"Sure." I reached out, stroked his arm. "What were you doing last night?"

"While you were confronting the real kidnapper?" Jack looked at me darkly. "Well, sweetheart, I was rear-ending your soon-to-be brother-in-law."

"What?"

"I decided the only way to look inside the car trunks—which, if you'll remember, was your suggestion—was to have a little accident with the cars involved. It would be reasonable to look in the trunk after that. I figured if I hit them just right, the trunk would open anyway."

"Did you hit Jess?"

"Yep."

"And Dill, too?"

"I was about to. But I was thinking I'd get whiplash, so I'd decided just to out-and-out break into Emory's. Then I got your call. I got to the O'Sheas' house just as your ex-boyfriend was pulling up. He cuffed me."

"He *what*?"

"I didn't want him going in ahead of me, so he cuffed me."

I didn't know what to say. I was trying not to smile.

"I better go get cleaned up," I told him. "You'll be there?"

"I brought my suit," he reminded me.

The only day it was possible for my parents not to cast me disapproving looks was Varena's wedding day. They were not excited that Jack had dropped me off in front of the house in broad daylight, with me wearing yesterday's clothes.

But in the melee of the wedding day—and the day before—it could be legitimately ignored.

I took a very long shower and brushed my teeth twice. To regain control of myself, I shaved my legs and armpits, plucked my eyebrows, spent ten or fifteen minutes putting on lotions and makeup.

It was only after I came into the kitchen in my bathrobe to drink some coffee that my mother spotted the bruise.

She put her own mug down with a clunk.

"Your neck, Lily."

I looked in a little mirror in the hall outside the kitchen. My neck had a spectacular dark bruise.

"Emory," I explained, for the first time noticing how hoarse my voice was. I touched the dark splotch. Sore. Very sore.

"It's OK," I said, "really. Just need to drink some-thing hot."

And that's all we said about the night before.

It was the best luck I ever had, that day being Varena's wedding day.

And the next morning, Christmas Day, I drove home to Shakespeare.

I thought during the drive: I thought what would become of the baby, Jane, whom Eve (I had to think of her as Eve Osborn) regarded as her sister. I wondered what would happen in the days to come, when the Macklesbys would finally get to put their arms around their daughter. I wondered when I'd have to go back to testify at Emory's trial. It gave me the cold shakes, thinking of going back to Bartley again, but I would feel more amenable when the time was closer, I hoped.

I didn't have to talk to anyone or listen to anyone for four whole hours.

The tatty outskirts of Shakespeare were so welcome to my eyes that I almost cried.

The decorations, the smoke coming out of the chimneys, the empty lawns and streets: Today was Christmas.

If my friend Dr. Carrie Thrush had remembered, the turkey would be thawed and waiting to be put in the oven.

And Jack, having detoured to Little Rock to pick up some more clothes, was on his way.

The presents I'd bought him were wrapped and in my closet. The spinach Madeleine, the sweet potato casserole, and the cranberry sauce were in the freezer.

I shed the past as I pulled into my own driveway.

I would have a Shakespeare Christmas.